# West of Cheyenne

# West of Cheyenne

## LEE HOFFMAN

**Sagebrush**
Large Print Westerns

**Library of Congress Cataloging in Publication Data**

Hoffman, Lee.
   West of Cheyenne / Lee Hoffman.
      p. (large print)   cm.
   ISBN 1-57490-111-7 (alk. paper)
   1. Large type books.  I. Title.
[PS3558.O346W4   1997]
813'.52—dc21                          96-52577
                                               CIP

Cataloguing in Publication Data is available from
the British Library and the National Library of Australia.

**Sagebrush Large Print Westerns** are published in the United States
and Canada by Thomas T. Beeler, Publisher, Box 659, Hampton
Falls, New Hampshire 03844-0659. ISBN 1-57490-111-7

Published in the United Kingdom, Eire, and the Republic of South
Africa by Isis Publishing Ltd, 7 Centremead, Osney Mead, Oxford
OX2 0ES  England. ISBN 0-7531-5542-7

Published in Australia and New Zealand by Australian Large Print
Audio & Video Pty Ltd, 17 Mohr Street, Tullamarine, Victoria, 3043,
Australia. ISBN 1-86340-693-X

Manufactured in the United States of America

# West of Cheyenne

# CHAPTER 1

WINTER WAS SUPPOSED TO BE OVER, BUT APPARENTLY the plains of Nebraska hadn't got the word yet. The wind that swept down off them had a feel of ice in it. Snow still lay thick on the ground, with the dry tips of brush poking through it like a beard stubble. The sun that barely cleared the eastern rim didn't look strong enough to help any.

Huddling with his back to the wind, the lone man held open the blanket he had draped over his shoulders. It sheltered the small fire and caught some of the heat for him. The smoke and the scent of the roasting chicken rose into his face.

It was a fine smell. Even the icy winds had a good smell to them But he didn't like this damned open country. He felt naked and vulnerable crouching in the shallow draw with bare land rolling off in every direction. Still, it was a hell of a lot better than the city had been.

Where he was, he could hear sounds from the Omaha railroad yards, but they lay downwind and out of his sight behind the rim of the draw. He was glad of that. He hoped he'd had his last of high walls, small close rooms, and stinking mobs of men packed together like pigs in a pen.

*Someone was coming.* Startled, he listened to the crunching of footsteps. Apprehension crept along the back of his neck. It was more than just one man, he thought. And coming toward him. They'd likely seen the smoke,maybe smelled his food. For an instant he was afraid.

1

As the long shadows fell into the draw, he reminded himself that he didn't have to stay still or silent. He could fight back if he needed to. And there was a sharp-honed-knife sheathed on his belt, easy at hand. Cautiously, he looked up.

Two men stood on the rim of the draw. One, in a wide-brimmed hat and blanket coat, had a saddle slung over his shoulder. It was a heavy, tangled-looking contraption with a lot of rigging and flapping skirts. He'd seen outfits like that and men dressed that way around the stock pens in Omaha. Cowboys, they were called.

The other, bigger man was wrapped in a greatcoat and had a slouch hat pulled low over his face. It, along with his dark, full beard, masked him.

The cowboy spoke, "Howdy. Mind if we step down and set a spell?"

He had a drawl that brought back damned unpleasant memories of Georgia. For a long silent moment the man at the fire gazed coldly at him.

"All right," he answered at last, but there was no sound of welcome in the curt grunt.

The cowboy looked surprised by the tone of voice, and a little uncomfortable. But the other one scrambled down and squatted to sniff at the cooking chicken. The cowboy followed then, and grinned crookedly. "I'm Cully. This here is Jasper."

Silence hung cold and harsh again before the man at the fire offered a response. "Hawkins," he muttered, biting the word off as if it were more than he'd wanted to say.

Jasper eyed the chicken, then looked at Hawkins. "That's a big bird."

He got no reaction but the steady return of his gaze.

Resentfully, he added, "A lot for one man to eat alone. You pluck it from behind some fence around here?"

"Bought it. And paid for it. In Omaha. At a butcher shop," Hawkins said. He sounded as if he expected them to demand to see a bill of sale.

"It sure does smell good," Cully said hopefully. He waited for an invitation that didn't come.

Hawkins understood their hints well enough. And he understood hunger. Carefully, he considered. Food was something a man didn't part with casually. The right of ownership was his. He was entitled to fight for it if need be. But he had to admit that the chicken was a big one. Left alone, he knew he'd gnaw every string of meat off its bones. Stuff himself too full to move comfortably. Maybe even make himself sick. That wouldn't be a sensible thing to do. He reminded himself that when he was hungry again, there'd be food for the buying. He had coin in his pocket, good hard money.

Weighing his thoughts, he asked the obvious. "You're hungry?"

"Hollow and pure empty to the boot heels," Cully said, grinning.

"And you got no money?"

"Cold stony-broke."

Jasper scowled. "You don't mean to charge us for a bite of food?"

Reluctantly, Hawkins shook his head. "I s'pose there's enough to share."

"That's better," Jasper said, sounding like he thought it was his due.

Sideways, without looking directly at him, Hawkins studied him. He'd met this kind before. He'd helped to hang a few once, and afterward had used pieces of the gallows to build a meager cook fire.

3

The cowboy didn't look to be the same kind, even if he did have a drawl like a Johnny Reb. His face was open and friendly. The scantiness of his sandy moustache, the freckles across his stubby nose, and the wide blue eyes gave him a look more like a little boy than a grown man.

Wistfully, he asked, "It's about cooked, ain't it?"

Hawkins nodded. As he reached toward the sheath on his belt, Jasper jerked open a clasp knife and grabbed for a drumstick. Hawkins watched him with cold resentment. The bird was *his*—the divvying up *his* right. But he said nothing. It wasn't until Jasper'd finished hacking off the leg and sat back to bite into it that he drew his sheath knife and sliced off the other one.

Impulsively, he held it out to the cowboy. But as Cully took it from him, the impulse passed. He felt resentful again as he watched the cowboy sink his teeth into the juicy meat.

This was *his* food. They had no right to come making demands on him for a share of it. They had no right to come intruding on him at all. He'd learned the hard way to live with just his own company. Now he was used to it and satisfied with it. He didn't want these strangers around him.

Sociably, Cully said, "I've been off wintering in the big city."

"Which one?" Jasper asked through a mouthful of meat.

"Omaha. Going back to Wyoming Territory now. Got to be there in time for spring hiring on the ranches."

"Omaha ain't much of a city," Jasper muttered. "New York or San Francisco, or maybe New Orleans—those are cities."

"What about Chicago?" Cully asked him.

4

He grunted scornfully.

"I hear it's all built back now. I plan to go see it next winter. Gonna fill my poke and catch the cars out with the beeves in the fall. Came out that way this time, prodding beeves. Meant to go to Chicago, but I got off at Omaha and that's about as far as I got." The cowboy smiled at some recollection. "Omaha ain't a bad town at all."

Off in the railroad yards, a steam whistle gave a sharp blast. Hawkins looked toward it. From where he crouched, he couldn't see over the rim of the draw. As he rose to his feet, Cully asked him, "You heading west?"

He nodded. Standing, he could see the track. In the distance puffs of smoke and white clouds of steam rose above the tops of the buildings in the yards.

"Got plenty of time yet," Cully said. "Engine makes a lot of noise in the yard 'fore she starts out. Goes real slow through them switches. Don't pick up much till she's way past here. You've rode the cars before, ain't you?"

"Not of my own will," Hawkins mumbled.

"Huh?"

"What do you mean?" Jasper said. He waited a moment, then asked, "Where is it you've been on the cars?"

Hawkins didn't want to answer. He didn't want to talk to these men at all. But he felt as if something unseen forced him to it. He counted off the places. "Andersonville, Blackshear, and Savannah in Georgia. Joliet in Illinois. And here."

"Ain't Andersonville that place where the Rebs had the prison camp?" Jasper asked.

Hawkins nodded.

5

"That where you was?"

"You ain't a Yankee?" Cully asked him.

"Been one."

The cowboy looked puzzled. He thought on it, then shrugged. "I've heard tell of Savannah, but not that Blackshear place."

"They had another prisoner camp there for a while," Hawkins said. The words came without his thinking about them first. That startled and vaguely frightened him.

Jasper asked, "What's at Joliet?"

"It's a place in Illinois."

"Near to Chicago?" Cully put in.

"Not too far."

"I sure would like to get to Chicago." He smiled to himself dreamily. Then, as if it were something important he'd almost forgotten, he added, "I'm from Texas myself. Southeast Texas."

Hawkins looked at him coldly. "Reb?"

"By upbringing. Was a mite too young for soldiering myself, but I had lots of kin what did it." For a moment he seemed proud of it. But his grin faded under Hawkins' steady gaze. He looked uncertain, then guiltily apologetic. He mumbled, "I reckon I heard some about that Andersonville place."

Without replying, Hawkins turned to stare toward the rails again. As much as he dreaded catching the cars, he wished to hell the train would come. He wanted to get away from these two.

He stood squinting against the sunlight on his face. There was some warmth in it, after all. Pleasant warmth. After a moment he shoved back his hat, then ran his hand along his jaw. He'd laid out for the night, and it had been too cold this morning for shaving or much

6

washing. But he'd had his chin scraped close in Omaha yesterday. There wasn't much stubble yet. Wouldn't be enough to bother him for another day or two. After that, though, the whiskers would be getting long enough to remind him of the gnawing pests that could move into an unkempt beard and hair.

He thought of open sores with maggots squirming m them.

"You gonna eat any more of this chicken?" Cully called. He wheeled back, wondering how he could have forgotten the food. He'd barely tasted it. These strangers had him shaken up and confused. Why the devil did they have to come prowling around here plaguing him like this?

Squatting, he hacked a chuck of meat off the bird and stuffed it into his mouth. The two of them had left plenty on the carcass for him, but he resented the amount they'd taken. He chewed hurriedly, swallowed hard, and tore loose another piece. As he ate, he was uncomfortably aware of the probing, hooded way Jasper watched him.

Cully was watching him, too, but with an open curiosity. Seeming somehow concerned, the cowboy said, "Work ain't too hard come by out West this time of year. Wyoming's getting to be real big cattle country, and the ranchers will be hiring on for the spring cow-hunting. If you're looking for work—can you ride a horse decent?"

"Used to." Hawkins grunted. "Ain't been on one for a long while, though." He bit off another piece of chicken, wondering how he'd come to speak out that way. He had a strange feeling, as if there were a lot of things in him that wanted saying out. He didn't know what they might be, though. And he was damned distrustful of

7

talking, anyway.

Cully suggested, "There's other kinds of work, too. 'Specially if you got some learning in a trade."

"You got a trade?" Jasper said, his voice sharp-edged and prying.

Hawkins sighed. He didn't want to talk. But he answered, "Can make shoes, I s'pose."

Cully studied on that. "How 'bout boots? Like these?" He thrust out a foot. Hawkins looked at the boot. It was an odd pattern to him. A band of red leather circled the top of it and was cut out in the shape of a star to show yellow leather underneath. Tugs hung down the sides. The toes were squared off, and the heels were high, sloping in under the instep. They didn't look very comfortable for walking.

"Don't mean to work at cobbling," he said. He'd damned well had his fill of it. And the memories that went with it.

Jasper eyed him with a vaguely smug expression, as if he thought he'd found some hidden secret. "What do you mean to work at?"

Hawkins didn't know. He returned Jasper's gaze coldly.

"There's other ways to make a living besides you *work* for it, ain't there?" Hints of ugly insinuation curled Jasper's voice.

Cully interrupted, trying to change the subject. "It ain't hard getting onto the cars up yonder. If a brakeman sees you, just slip him four bits and he won't bother you. If you got four bits."

"What's four bits?" Hawkins asked.

Cully looked surprised. "Fifty cents."

"That's a lot of money."

"It's better'n getting hit with a club and throwed off

the cars."

Jasper was studying Hawkins with a sneering grin. "I know what's wrong with you. You're not long out of prison, ain't you?"

"What the hell business is it of yours?" Hawkins snapped.

Cully grunted, eying Hawkins in curious question. But Jasper looked happy, like he had just about succeeded in something he wanted real bad. He swung to his feet. "Don't try talking tough at me, jailbird."

Motionless, Hawkins stared at him. It was hard to break habits that had been beaten in. But it was his right now, he told himself. He had the papers to prove it.

Rising slowly, he closed his hands into fists at his sides. He was tall and lean, too lean for his bone. The light coat he wore hung loose at the shoulders. He looked about as dangerous as a scarecrow.

Jasper's grid broadened crookedly. He fairly glowed. "Don't *act* tough at me either, jailbird."

The angers and hatreds in Hawkins had been smoldering, suppressed for long years. He thought of the men like this he'd known. Guards who took their pleasure in pushing men around, trash who kept proving themselves by making others worse off than they were, men who acted like anything they wanted was their rightful due, no matter what, who demanded and took by force. Men who were just plain mean. He gazed at Jasper, knowing him and hating him.

As Hawkins had risen, Jasper'd cocked clenched fists. But now he thought he read fear in Hawkins' hesitation. Smirking, he opened a hand and swung it. His palm struck Hawkins' cheek, the sound a flat crack in the morning stillness.

Anger sprang to flame. Ducking his head, Hawkins

9

drove toward Jasper. His first blow slammed at Jasper's gut, the second up under the jaw.

Jasper hadn't expected the fists or the force behind them. He gasped, jerking up his own hands. His guard was too high. Hawkins swung under, into the gut again. His knuckles bit through the muffling thickness of the greatcoat into Jasper's belly. And the other hand rammed bone-hard into Jasper's face.

The nose bent under the blow. Hot blood spewed from it, dribbling down Jasper's chin. He backed, trying to collect himself. But Hawkins followed furiously, fist and fist, hammering.

There was a sudden wild pleasure in it that overwhelmed Hawkins. He felt like hollering, the way the men had when he'd ridden the near wheeler in front of a twelve-pound Napoleon. The memories jumped vividly into his mind. The team thundering at full gallop, hauling well over half a ton of gun and caisson frantically behind it, slamming over the rutted roads with a fierce jangling of chains and clatter of wheels.

It would have been impossible to swerve or stop that force suddenly, so the riders had shouted in warning. Anyone in the road had to jump quick or be ridden down. The foot soldiers had cursed the horse artillery for that, the way Jasper cursed Hawkins now.

The shouting had been more than just warning. It was wildness, too. At full gallop, the horses hitched to the caisson and cannon were barely under control. The men on them, trying to handle them and their burden, had known the fine edge of disaster they'd ridden. The pounding thunder of the hoofs had echoed in their blood. They'd clung to the reins, straining for control, shouting their wild warnings.

Hawkins held no rein now. The long-banked sparks

had become fire. It burned in his blood as he slammed his fists at this man he hated. The anger that had been held subdued for so long had burst free. It gave him a fierce momentum. He couldn't have swerved or stopped suddenly. He didn't want to.

Jasper's curses turned to gasps and grunts as he tried desperately to defend himself against the fury he'd called onto himself. The greatcoat hindered him. It absorbed some force from the blows that struck him, but it interfered with his own movements. He tried to land his fist in Hawkins' belly, but the coat cramped his shoulders. His knuckles hit Hawkins in the ribs, sliding askew. Hawkins didn't even seem aware of the blows.

But the furious strength in him was waning. It had been too long since he'd fought last. Shopwork and the lock step didn't keep muscles hard or reflexes honed. He was tiring fast, struggling for breath. He jerked back and paused to haul air into his lungs.

Jasper grabbed at the respite. Staggering, he turned away. He turned full circle. As he came to face Hawkins again, there was something clutched in his hand. Something small and dark and double-barreled.

Hawkins recognized it for a derringer. It pointed straight at his chest. Reluctantly, he lifted his hands.

Jasper's whole body heaved as he sucked breath. Blood smeared his face and dripped from his chin. His mouth twisted into a sneer as he gazed at Hawkins.

He meant to kill, and he wallowed in this moment of anticipation. Hawkins could read that easily in his face.

It was a hell of a way for things to work out—to die suddenly before he got where he was going—or even knew where he was headed. It seemed like all the business of growing up, all the years of just surviving, had been pure waste. Hawkins looked at the gun, feeling cheated. He'd have saved himself a lot of trouble if he'd just gotten killed in the war.

He was suddenly aware of the cowboy.

Cully'd been standing by, watching the fight with a frown of disapproval. But at the sight of the pistol he caught a sharp breath and scowled. Glancing toward him, Hawkins met his narrowing eyes. The cowboy nodded slightly. Hawkins saw the beginning of a move. Understanding—reacting—he lunged.

With a high-pitched yelp, Cully scooped up the hulk of the chicken. He flung it at Jasper.

Flinching, Jasper triggered the derringer.

Hawkins heard the blast and felt the hat snatched off his head. He saw recoil rock the pistol upward in Jasper's hand. He came up under the hand, grappling the wrist.

Jasper staggered back, pulling against the sudden weight on his arm. Jerkily, he raised his free hand to slam it down into Hawkins' face.

Hawkins heard a thud and a grunt. He felt the taut muscles of Jasper's arm ease. Jasper tottered, spilling to the ground.

As he'd released his grip, Hawkins was off-balance. He fell to his knees. He looked up. Cully stood just behind the downed man. There was a very large revolver in his hand and an uncertain expression on his face.

He mumbled, "Just buffaloed him. He'll wake up again right pert."

"I thought he was your friend," Hawkins said.

"No," Cully drawled. His coat was unbuttoned, showing the bright blue of his shirt and a big silver buckle on a wide belt. Shoving back the coat skirt, he dropped the revolver into a holster on the belt. He began fingering the buttons closed again. "No, I only just met him this morning on my way past the freight yards. Didn't owe him nothing. You, though—you shared grub with me. I'm obliged for that."

Hawkins got slowly to his feet. He felt empty and exhausted. There was something that should be said, but he couldn't shape it, even for himself. He picked up his hat. There was a ragged hole in the brim. He dusted it against his thigh, turning his back to Cully as he did it.

Thoughts were a confused jumble. As he tried to sort them, he glanced toward the sun. It was hazed over by a streamer of dark smoke from the rail yards. Behind the yards, Omaha was a tumble of ugly black blocks against the morning sky. Everything else was across the river. The memories—the things remembered—were all back there.

He ran a hand through his hair before he put on the hat. Despite the cold winds, there was sweat on his face. He was aware of knowing that life was something he wanted to hang on to. In a way it was just beginning. He was anxious to find out where it might lead to. And hopeful that maybe it would go someplace that he wanted to be.

From the distance, he heard the sound of an engine hissing sharply, then beginning to move with a slow pounding rumble.

"That might be the cars west," Cully said softly.

Hawkins turned toward him and grinned.

For an instant the cowboy looked surprised, as if he hadn't thought Hawkins could grin. And Hawkins was surprised himself.

Feeling strangely embarrassed, he bent to roll up his blanket. He slung it, Reb style, over his shoulder and picked up his kit. Mumbling, he said, "Maybe we ought to get over to the rails."

Cully nodded and hefted his saddle. As he started walking, Hawkins hesitated. There was still meat on the carcass of the chicken. He knew it was foolish, but he picked it up and brushed at the dirt on it. Looking over his shoulder, Cully asked, "You really want that thing?"

Hawkins studied on it, trying to understand why he clung to it. The time of hunger—of damned desperate hunger when a man would gnaw leaves or bark or anything he could lay his hands on—was past. Long past. Why the hell did it hang on his shoulders, riding him this way?

Struggling with himself to do it, he dropped the chicken and wiped his greasy fingers on his pants leg.

"Come on," Cully said. "That Jasper'll be waking up any minute."

Hawkins nodded and started after him. But he couldn't help glancing back toward the abandoned piece of meat and bones. Over the rim of the draw, he glimpsed Jasper stirring. He hoped the train would come before the man could catch up with them. He wanted to get away from that kind. He wanted to get away from a damned lot of things.

# CHAPTER 2

GRUNTING AND MUMBLING TO ITSELF, THE TRAIN passed the last switch. It was beginning to gradually pick up speed as it reached the point where Hawkins and Cully crouched waiting.

They ran alongside, pacing it. Grabbing for the rungs at the side of a freight car, Hawkins hauled himself up. As soon as he'd cleared the lowest rungs, Cully caught

14

at one. Hawkins glanced down at him, glad they'd both gotten onto the same car.

There was a brakeman trotting along the catwalk toward them, waving his bullystick. He scowled and raised it in threat.

Clinging to the grab iron, Hawkins fished a dollar out of his pocket. He held it up.

The brakeman squatted, balancing on the rocking car with the skill of long practice. When he reached for the money, Hawkins gave a jerk of his head toward Cully.

The brakeman nodded agreement as he took the coin. Hollering to be heard above the rising clamor of the wheels, he told Hawkins, "Next car up. Door's open on this side."

The car swayed and jolted as Hawkins climbed onto the top of it. He gripped the edge, holding his other hand out. He caught the saddle as Cully hefted it, and hauled it up. Cully followed it.

They rested a moment, then jumped the gap between the cars and made their way along the precarious catwalk. It was a damnsight trickier than riding an artillery horse, Hawkins thought. He glanced back at the brakeman who ambled along the cars as if he were out for a Sunday stroll. The world seemed to be full of men who knew what they were doing. He watched the brakeman with a vague envy.

Cully stretched out on his stomach, hanging his head over the side of the car to check the door. He swung himself into the empty car and held up his hands to catch the saddle.

Hawkins dropped it to him, then lowered himself. He landed on his feet inside the car. Leaning his back against the wall, he dragged a deep breath. His heart was hammering wildly against his ribs. It wasn't the fear of physical danger that he felt, but uncertainty. He'd made it this far. What next?

Cully grinned at him.

It occurred to him that he'd made a friend. And that was an unsettling thought, too.

The empty boxcar was hardly warm inside, but it was more comfortable than the open plain had been. Cully settled his saddle on the floor and sat down beside it, leaning his back against the wall. He rubbed his hands together, flexed his fingers, and sighed, relaxing.

It took Hawkins awhile longer to catch breath and ease the tension that he felt enough to sit down. Resting his arms on his knees, he looked at his hands. They were trembling slightly.

"Cold?" Cully asked him.

He nodded, though he knew that wasn't the reason.

"I'm obliged to you," the cowboy said. "I'll pay you back that four bits when I get working and collect my wage."

Hawkins gave him no answer.

Cully sat silent awhile, then tried again to strike up a conversation. "Can you spare the money that long? If you need it right quick, I got friends around Cheyenne I can borrow off."

"I got enough," Hawkins muttered. Suddenly he felt a need to explain. He couldn't understand why, but the feeling was there.

Resentfully, as if something compelled him to it, he said, "'Fore they arrested me, I'd won a piece of money in a gambling game. When they let me go, they give me back my belongings, and some of it was still there."

"Only some of it?"

He nodded.

"What happened to the rest?"

16

"Somebody took it, I s'pose."

"You don't know who?"

"Likely somebody working for the prison."

Curious, Cully asked, "Wasn't there no way you could get it back?"

"No."

He shook his head in disapproval. "It ain't fair to steal off a man when he ain't got a way to get back at you."

"If a man's got something, there's always somebody looking to steal it off him," Hawkins said. "The worse off he is, the quicker they'll do it."

Cully sighed sadly. "Wolves always go for a lame calf, I reckon. It ain't fair, though."

What was fair never seemed to matter much, Hawkins thought. He looked at his hands again. They weren't exactly trembling now, but they weren't quite steady, either.

"Where you planning to get off?" the cowboy asked him.

"Dunno."

"Ain't you going no place in particular?"

He shook his head.

"I'm getting off at Cheyenne City. Worked to a ranch near there last year. For a man name of Starrett. Reckon he'll hire me on again this year. I'll put in a word for you if you want to try for a job there."

"No. There's something I've got to do."

"Only you don't know *where?*" Cully raised a brow in question.

"I'm looking for somebody," Hawkins owned. "I don't know where he is right now, but only that he worked on building this railroad."

"What are you looking for him for?"

There was a hint of uneasiness in the cowboy's voice.

17

It triggered the sense of distrust in Hawkins. He felt apprehension drawing taut along his spine again.

Dammit, this man had swept in on him like a flank attack, making friends while he was off guard. He hadn't asked for a friend. Hadn't wanted one. But the cowboy had tricked him and got him to talking away like a pot boiling over.

He glared resentfully at Cully.

"I reckon it ain't none of my business," the cowboy muttered, looking away.

Hawkins said nothing.

Cully picked up the end of a saddle string. He fingered it, frowning at it. His mouth shaped several words before he gave them voice.

"It's just kinda—well, sometimes a man's looking for somebody and he's got a real fine reason. But sometimes he's purely looking for trouble. I dunno. But maybe it ain't good. I mean with you out of jail and all. Maybe it'd be better if you'd forget it and come on up to Starrett's with me. Likely he'd give you work all right. Ain't no point in *hunting* trouble. A man can get more than enough of that without he halfway tries."

"Dammit, what do you think you're doing!" Hawkins snapped. The words came unplanned and uncontrolled. "What gives you call to be friends with me!"

Cully eyed him in bewilderment. "I dunno."

"You got no right! You got no claim on me!"

"Didn't mean to make no claim on you," he mumbled, twisting the saddle string around his finger. "If there's any claim at all, it's the other way bound. Was *you* as shared your grub and coin with *me*. It's me as owes you."

Hawkins eased himself back. A sense of guilt washed at his anger. He could recall a time when he'd had friends. He could remember when it had been a good thing—something he'd wanted. But he couldn't recapture the feeling.

The guilt and anger mingled in him, confusing him. He heard himself saying, "It's my brother I'm looking for. I ain't seen him since early in the war. I need—need to find him."

Looking up again, Cully grinned as if he'd taken the words for an apology. It occurred to Hawkins that maybe they were. He was too confused inside to make sense of himself.

"You know what name he's going by?" Cully asked him. "I know some of the folk settled around Cheyenne who worked on the railroad. Some around Laramie and Garrison and Rock Creek, too."

"Hawkins, same as me, I s'pose. Jacob Hawkins. Don't know no reason he'd of changed it."

"Lot of people do it. Jacob Hawkins. Sounds kinda familiar. Maybe—yeah, feller I set into card games with a few times. Hawkins might of been his name. Mostly folks called him Hawk. He was dark-headed like you. Dark-bearded." The cowboy peered at him, studying on it. "Yeah, I reckon he might of looked a fair bit like you. Fleshier, though. Heavier-set. But likely it was him, all right."

Hawkins swallowed at the rising sense of excitement. He didn't dare let himself really believe that Cully was rights. He could hope, though. He asked, "Where was this?"

"Cheyenne City. It's where I'm getting off."

"I'll get off with you."

"Might be he's moved on by now," Cully warned him. "Lot of fellers don't stay put long."

"Wherever he is, I'll find him," he said softly. There

19

was the one thing he was certain of. He'd find Jake. He had to.

What with stopping at depots all along the way and laying over on a siding for a good while to let a fancy passenger train go past, it had come twilight of the second day and Cheyenne still wasn't within sight.

Hawkins had the boxcar door part way open. He stood leaning against it, with the cold wind in his face, watching ahead for some sign of the city.

He could see ragged peaks silhouetted against the sunset, but nothing that looked like lamplight or buildings. It had to show soon, he thought as he squinted against the wind. The tension of waiting was growing in him with every jolting turn of the wheels.

Cully was talking. He'd been doing that a lot, telling stories about things he'd done and places he'd been. Mostly Hawkins had taken pleasure in listening, trying to make pictures in his mind to fit them. Cully talked about a lot of things he'd never seen, some he'd never even heard of. That hadn't surprised him, though.

But now he hadn't the patience for listening. The voice, pitched high and loud to be heard over the rumble of the train, rasped painfully at his tight-drawn nerves. Suddenly he couldn't stand it any more. Wheeling, he snapped, "Shut up!"

Cully stopped in mid-word.

None of the faint twilight filtered into the car. Hawkins couldn't see the cowboy. He gazed into darkness, sensing that he'd shouted too harshly. It hadn't been called for. It was wrong.

"You know, you're a hell of a hard man to get along with," Cully said.

Hawkins nodded to himself. He'd have to learn

different if he hoped to survive in this strange new world, he thought. Vaguely apologetic, he mumbled, "I ain't used to much talk."

"Lot of the time I got nobody to talk to," Cully answered in a like tone. "When I get somebody as will listen, I reckon I kinda run off at the mouth."

"I just ain't used to it." Hawkins had that uncomfortable feeling that he had to explain himself again. He added, "You ain't s'pose to talk none in prison."

"Never?"

"Not ever. Not to nobody. Except less a guard asks you something outright, and it sure ain't often they do that."

"What are you s'pose to do?" Cully asked curiously.

"Just work."

"You can't work all the time."

"When you ain't working, you're locked up in a cell about the size of a coffin. You're all alone, and you're s'posed to think on your sin and repent it."

"Did you?"

Hawkins shook his head. "I didn't figure I'd done a sin. Not the way they meant."

From the sound of his voice, Cully was embarrassed to be asking such questions, but too interested to hold back. "What was you s'posed to have done?"

"I didn't figure it was a sin," Hawkins repeated. He still didn't feel it was, but he had to own to himself that it had been a crime under the law. He felt shamed by that.

The Hawkinses had always been honest, law-'biding folk. *He* was the one who'd got the family name put down for a crime and marked guilty. He didn't want to talk about it. He didn't even want to think about it. But he couldn't stop himself of that.

Silently he turned away from the question to stare through the open door. After a long while, he muttered into the wind, "I killed a man."

There was no response. He didn't know whether Cully had heard him or not. But, oddly, he felt better for having said it.

The last traces of the sunset had faded and the sky was crazy with stars when finally he spotted lamplight in the distance.

"There it is!" he hollered.

Cully got up and came to look. "Yeah, that's it. You know the fare you paid ain't quite good all the way to the depot. We got to get off the cars 'fore they get slam into town. Jump soon as they've slowed down enough."

"You say when," Hawkins whispered, hoarse with anticipation. He didn't trust himself to know the right time. He felt too close to his goal, too knotted with anxiety, to trust his own judgment of anything. He was depending on Cully. Realizing that, he felt overwhelmed with a sense of fresh-foaled helplessness. Under his breath he muttered a curse, not sure whether it was meant for the cowboy or himself.

The brakes gave sharp squeals as the train began to slow. Ahead, the lights were vivid, lining out windows and shaping black boxes of buildings. Hawkins watched them grow more distinct. He could feel the pace of the car easing.

"Now!" Cully grunted.

Clinging to his kit, Hawkins flung himself off the train. He landed, crumpling, rolling in the mud at trackside. He lay still, listening to the rattle of the wheel trucks running past. A thud and grunt and the sounds of scrambling told him Cully had jumped not far away.

22

He rested a moment longer, drawing breath and taking count of himself. He'd already had a few sore and aching spots from that fight with Jasper. It felt like he'd added a few new bruises.

"Hawk? You all right?" Cully called.

He propped himself up and answered, "Sure."

Cully had gotten to his feet. Hawkins could see him against the sky glow. He didn't look any the worse for having leaped off the moving car. Hawkins watched him heave the saddle over his shoulder.

"Come on, let's get into town," he said.

Hawkins dragged himself up and shouldered his kit. He felt a mild twinge of pain in one knee, as if he'd twisted it in the fall. The pain didn't bother him, though. He barely noticed it as he fell in beside Cully, matching his long stride.

The train was already pulled up at the depot, stopped still and hissing to itself, when they got there. As they came up, a man threw a switch and it began to puff, rolling slowly backward and turning. They had to wait for it to get past.

Watching the cars, Cully said, "You know that feller Jasper was heading for Cheyenne, too. Likely he'll be in on tomorrow's train. You'd better keep an eye out for him. He ain't the forgiving kind."

"Maybe *you'd* better keep an eye out, too. *You're* the one who cracked him over the skull."

"I expect he'll hold you to blame for it, though," he answered. "Anyway, I don't reckon I'll be around town long. Be on my way up to Starrett's tomorrow to see about work. You sure you don't want to come along?"

"I'm sure."

"Where'm I gonna find you to pay you back that four bits?"

"Forget it," Hawkins muttered.

The engine chugged past them. Ahead, a row of buildings, mostly square-fronted and one-storied, faced onto a wide street running alongside the main track. Windows blazed with light, and there were lanterns hung out along the plank walk.

"Lets us head for a saloon," Cully said. "Might be I could borrow enough money somewheres to buy you a drink."

Hawkins rubbed his knuckles at the scruff on his jaw. The stubble of beard was getting too long, and the mud from the backside caked in his clothes. The memories seemed too real.

"I got to get clean first," he said. "You think maybe there's a barbershop still open around here?"

"Sure. Right up that way." Cully pointed past the dark looming sheds of the railroad yard. Then he aimed his finger at a brightly lit saloon up the street. "I'll be at the Palace over yonder. You come on over, meet me there?"

A promise was an obligation. Hawkins didn't want obligations, not even such a simple one as this. He muttered, "Maybe."

Cully hesitated, then shrugged. As he started uproad, he called, "I'll see you."

For a moment Hawkins stood watching him and studying over the town. It wasn't as big as Omaha, but it was still too large to suit his feelings. He didn't want to go into it or have doors closing behind him. He didn't want to mix with other men, smelling their stink and being hammered at by their voices. But he had to, if he meant to find Jake.

It'd be easier after he'd got bathed and trimmed, he told himself. Face the barbershop first, then the rest of it. Resettling the blanket rolled over his shoulder, he started walking in the direction Cully had pointed. He stayed to the dark sidle of the street, in the protection of the shadows,

The footstep was furtive. The sound of it sent a sharp chill along his spine. His hand darted under the coat for the sheath knife as he started to turn.

Something glanced against the side of his head. It slammed down hard onto his left shoulder. Hard enough to have broken bone if the blanket hadn't muffled its force.

The blow staggered him. He stumbled and felt himself falling. But the knife was in his hand, clear of the coat. Twisting as he fell, he swung it.

The back of his shoulder hit against a wall. It kept him from falling farther. For a moment, he leaned against it, shifting the knife in his hand. He'd felt the point tick something when he'd swung. He gripped it, ready to lunge.

It looked like a bear hulking between him and the lights of the street. But bears didn't carry clubs. This was a man bundled in a cloak or greatcoat, holding a hefty stick of some kind. And swinging it again.

Hawkins' left arm was numbed from that blow on the shoulder. He flung it up awkwardly, ducking, as the club rammed toward his head.

The attacker's forearm struck across his, twisting him as he swung the knife. He felt the blade catch. It cut into thick cloth, snagging. He jerked it free.

The club lashed downward. But he was close to the attacker now. The blow angled against the back of his shoulder, a thud of pain but nothing that would hinder him. He didn't swing again. He drove the knife with his full weight behind it.

The blade bit and sank in. He felt the quiver of

25

shocked flesh against it—the wince—he heard the startled grunt of pain. The attacker jerked back off the knife, tottering. The club clattered to the ground.

As Hawkins lunged again, the man wheeled. Bending with both arms clutched to his body, he broke into a lurching run.

Hawkins plunged after him into the glow of the street lights. On the walks, men turned to stare. Someone started toward the man in the greatcoat. Someone else gave a sharp high shout of encouragement.

The attacker slowed. He staggered awkwardly, stopped, and turned to look helplessly at Hawkins. It was Jasper.

Hawkins caught himself in mid-stride. It was unnatural. Jasper couldn't have been back there at Omaha and here in Cheyenne both This wasn't a man but a devil. Or a wild fever dream. Startled, frightened by that thought, Hawkins stared at him.

Just as the man from the walk reached for Jasper's arm, Hawkins grabbed at the greatcoat. Clutching the front of it in his left hand, he lifted the knife to Jasper's throat.

"How?" he demanded.

Jasper's eyes were wide with fear and empty of understanding.

"Here—ahead of me," Hawkins asked breathlessly. "How? How'd you get here? You *are* here?"

Jasper nodded. He stammered, "Passenger train—faster—thought you'd be with that cowboy—"

Easing the blade back; Hawkins sighed with relief. The man was real. There was an explanation that made sense.

Someone behind him snapped, "What the hell's going on here?"

The one who offered support to Jasper answered, "Looks like some kind of a knife fight to me, Marshal."

*Marshal?* Hawkins wheeled toward the man who'd asked. He didn't see the man's face, only the bright metal star pinned to his coat.

"You'd better give me that knife, boy," the lawman said.

Hawkins stood motionless. The men from the walk were bunching around now. He could feel them crowding in, like high walls. He could smell them, unwashed, unshaven men with the odor of smoke clinging to them. The scents that seemed wrong were of whisky and coal oil. There'd been neither in Andersonville.

He gave a shake of his head, trying to separate the memories from the thing that was happening now.

"Give me the knife," the marshal repeated firmly.

The men were too close and the memories too strong. Submissively, Hawkins held the knife out on his open hand. He felt the loss, as if it were his life being snatched away, when the marshal took it from him.

Looking past him, the lawman called, "Somebody go chase up a doctor for that one. Lemme know how he's getting on."

Then he turned to Hawkins, closing a hand over his wrist. "Come on, boy. I'm gonna lock you up. We got *law* in this town now."

Hawkins shook his head. A sense of panic cramped his throat and twisted in his gut. He wanted to jerk back, to protest. He wanted to explain. It hadn't been his fault. Jasper had jumped him. He'd only fought back. He had the right . . .

But he didn't have the words.

"Come on, boy."

27

He yielded. Head hung and unspeaking, he followed the lawman.

# CHAPTER 3

HE WAS SILENT. THERE WERE QUESTIONS HE WANTED to ask, but he couldn't find the voice for them. The papers that said he was pardoned—that he had the rights of a man again—were meaningless. He was an object, sullen but obedient. He walked into the cell.

The door slammed shut behind him.

A lamp was burning low outside the door. Its thin light fell through the strap-iron grating. It made a pattern of wide-spaced squares on the floor. Hawkins stood, breaking the pattern with his shadow. As his eyes accepted the dim light, he could see the lumpy shape of a pallet in the corner.

It stunk of other men. It would be specked with pests and nits. For a long while he hesitated, but there was no alternative. Reluctantly he sat down on it. The seam rabbits would crawl into his clothes, he thought dully. There was no way to stop them.

Overwhelmed with an awareness of the dirt of two days traveling in the cars, he itched. The scruff of his beard was too long now, and it would get longer. Fleas and lice would bed in it. There'd be scabs, and sores that wouldn't heal and filth, and hunger.

He shook his head, knowing that he was confused. He kept mixing up the memories, losing track of which belonged where and when. The damned miserable, unbearable filth and hunger had belonged at Camp Sumter in Andersonville. And the war was over now, the camp gone, the commander judged, convicted, and executed. He clung to a certainty of that.

Prison had been different. There'd been clean water in prison and the chance to bathe almost every week. They'd kept his hair and beard cropped. The pests hadn't been too bad. And there'd been food every day, even if it was never quite enough.

He rubbed his hand over his face and told himself firmly that this wasn't Andersonville or the prison at Joliet, either one. He wasn't captured or sentenced. He hadn't done wrong in fighting back when Jasper attacked him. This time he'd speak up and make the jury understand. This time he wouldn't let the real things get all tangled up with the fever dreams.

Only the feverish fears were trying to force themselves onto him again. They tumbled in his mind, trying to tear away the certainties. Shivering, he struggled against them. But they crowded around him, looming like high walls. And he was hungry. So godawful hungry.

Footsteps. The dank of metal on metal. He rose and pressed his back against the far wall as the door swung. open.

"Come here," the marshal said.

Obediently he walked forward.

"You come in on the cars today?"

"Yes sir."

"Well, that train'll be pulling out again in about ten or fifteen minutes. You're gonna be on it. You're getting out of Cheyenne City, and you ain't coming back. You understand me?"

"Yes sir."

The marshal gestured toward his blanket and kit. "Pick 'em up, and I'll walk you over to the tracks."

He obeyed. The questions milled in his mind. He

29

wanted to ask about Jacob. He wanted desperately to know about the man he had cut. But he couldn't speak them. Silently, he gathered his gear and started for the door.

The lawman said nothing more, but followed behind, herding him toward the railroad yards. There were trainmen busy around the cars. A second engine was being backed up to the train. Someone atop a car swung a bright bull's-eye lantern.

A gun snapped twice and the lantern blinked out. The trainman cursed viciously.

"Damn them cowboys," the marshal muttered.

Hawkins kept walking. He was being herded toward the last car. It had a couple of windows and an open door that showed lamplight from inside. As a man started up through the door, the marshal called, "Hold on, 1 got some cargo for you."

The trainman turned. "What's that?"

"I want this freighted out of here." The marshal hooked a thumb toward Hawkins.

The trainman didn't seem surprised. He glanced at Hawkins and asked the marshal, "Anywhere in particular this time?"

"No, I don't give a damn where you drop him, long as it's far from this town."

"Six bits."

The marshal held out the coins. Taking them, the trainman eyed Hawkins. "Climb on board."

As he stepped up, the marshal called to him, "Don't you give a damn about that man you knifed?"

He looked back. "Yes sir."

"Well, he ain't hurt bad," the marshal grumbled, sounding disgusted. "And you're damned lucky of it."

Hawkins hesitated. Drawing a deep breath, he told

himself that this wasn't prison—he was free—he had rights. Hoarse-voiced, he asked, "Can I have my knife back?"

The marshal worked his mouth and spat. Reaching under his coat, he brought out the weapon. He tossed it, meaning it to stick into the doorframe.

Hawkins caught it by the hilt as it tumbled. Sliding it into the sheath on his belt, he muttered, "I'm obliged."

"You'll get the hell out of my town and *stay out,* you understand?" the lawman snapped at him.

He nodded, but he knew that he'd have to come back. This was the place Jake had been. And no matter what, he *had* to find Jake.

As the marshal stalked away, the trainman asked Hawkins, "Anywhere special you want to get off?"

"No."

"Not Sherman," the man muttered thoughtfully.

"They've give me hell for putting too many tramps off there already."

Hawkins licked his lips. The tentativeness of his voice made his words into questions. "I'm looking for somebody? For Jacob Hawkins?"

The trainman studied on him. "You some kin of Jake's?"

"Brother."

"Hell, yeah. You sure favor him all right! Me and Jake built this railroad together. Us and some other fellers. Used to buck the tiger together all along the track." Grinning broadly, the man thrust a thick hand toward him. Then the grin faded. "You ain't heard?"

He shook his head.

"Jake died. Back around Christmas."

The words slammed into him, tearing through him like shot. He stood staring, feeling the life drain out of his body.

"Got killed," the trainman was saying. "Left that poor little wife of his all alone."

"Wife?"

"Maybe you'd want to see her? She's working at the eating place in Garrison. I can let you off there."

Hawkins nodded slightly, but he wasn't sure. It was an too sudden and too unexpected. The confusion washed through him, and with it, the sense of hopelessness. He'd been counting on Jake. He'd *had* to find Jake. But Jake was dead.

West of Cheyenne the train climbed steeply, straining through the night. It made slow progress, groaning up the grade until it had at last reached Sherman Summit. Then it stopped and the extra engine was unhooked. There was more of a delay while some kind of minor repair was made.

Stretched out on the floor of the waycar, Hawkins tried to sleep. He drowsed, but the memories haunting his dreams would jerk him awake again. And lying there thinking wasn't much better. If Jake was dead, he was left without a goal. He didn't know where he was going, or even where to look for a direction. He'd been depending on Jake.

The cars finally rolled again. It was almost dawn when they halted at the Garrison depot. As Hawkins dropped off, the trainman called after him, wishing him luck. It seemed like a fool thing for the man to say. Hawkins felt beyond the reach of luck—good or bad. He was trapped somewhere between the nightmares and the world that was real, not able to escape one or reach the other. He strode away from the train feeling like a sleepwalker.

There were a few lit lanterns around the depot and

train, but the rest of the town was dark. Starlight barely suggested the row of buildings across the street from the track. The air was tainted with smoke from the engine, but there was a fresh smell to it, too. An odor of forests mingled with animal scents. He breathed deep of it, trying to ease the cramped tension in his chest.

The eastern sky gave only the faintest promise of the sunrise to come. He'd have to wait awhile before he could hunt for this unknown woman who'd been his brother's wife. He wasn't sure why he wanted to find her. But it was a thing to do, and he didn't know of anything else. In the lee of the depot building, he unrolled his blanket. Wrapping it around his shoulders, he sat down with his back against the wall.

He dozed, and in the dream he smelled the scorched smoke of the resiny southern pine, a smoke that had stained men's skins black and had seemed as if it would never wash away. He heard a dog growl and thought it was a hound close behind, hunting him through the swamp. They'd said the hounds were almost as hungry as the prisoners—that they'd tear a man apart if they caught up to him. He smelled cooking food and thought it was only a dream and he was so godawful hungry.

He woke suddenly. The sharp-angled light of the sun that sat over the eastern ridges burned into his eyes. As he squinted against it, something thudded into his leg and a voice snarled, "Hey, you can't sleep here. Get up."

Blinking, he looked at a man in a black suit. Bright metal glinted against the man's vest. For an instant he was afraid it was another lawman come to arrest him. But then he saw that the metal was a heavy gold watch chain.

"This is railroad property," the man was saying. "You can't sleep here."

He realized with deep relief that it was the station agent. As he began to roll his blanket again, he asked, "Is there a barbershop near here?"

The railroad man looked surprised. He studied on Hawkins curiously. His voice was a lot less harsh when he said "Beck Holley's place. He'll be opening up in an hour or so. Right across the street."

"What about an eating place? Where a Miz Hawkins might be working?"

"That's right across the street, too. In this town, everything is right across the street." He pulled out the watch at the end of the chain and looked at it. Then he glanced toward the sun. "They ought to be open right soon. Lot of the folks in town take breakfast there. The lodging house dining room."

"Obliged," Hawkins muttered, shouldering his gear. He turned toward the street.

The lodging house was almost directly in front of the depot. It was two stones high, with galleries across the width of each floor. The railings and shutters were whitewashed, sharp and clean looking against the red brick. A sign lettered in gold across the front read LODGING—MEALS—BOARDERS. It seemed to be the biggest, fanciest building in town. The places flanking it in a haphazard scatter were mostly just one story and built of planks.

He scanned a hardware store, a place advertising seed, feed, meats, and groceries, a couple of saloons, and a small post office. At the far end of the street, where it turned into a pair of wheel ruts, there was a barn almost as big as the lodging house. It had a rail pen behind it and a sign saying it was a livery stable.

The wheel ruts climbed a shallow slope toward a low ridge, then rose farther to disappear into woods. Off here and there houses speckled the slopes. Half-hidden behind a clump of trees, he could make out a building with a bell tower. A church or meeting house or school, he figured. Maybe all three. This was a right small town But even so, the square-fronted stores reminded him too much of walls and the air held too much of an odor of men.

He caught a scent of food cooking as he looked to the lodging house again. Smoke was curling out of an unseen chimney to the back of it. A well-dressed man ambled along the side of the street and up the steps onto the Lower gallery. Hawkins heard a small bell tinkle as the man opened the door and went on in.

He rubbed a hand against his whiskers, wishing the barbershop was open. Everything would be easier if only he could get cleaned up first. But the lodging house would be serving breakfast soon, and the barbershop wouldn't open for another hour or so. And he was damned hungry.

He headed across the street wondering what he'd say to his brother's widow if he found her. Maybe nothing.

Maybe he'd just take a meal and leave again quick without even looking for her.

The door tripped the bell as he pushed it open. He walked into a lobby fixed up like a sitting room. There were several sofas, a couple of small tables, and a stone fireplace in the back wall that was almost as tall as he was. No one was in the room. He looked around as he stood waiting.

Stuffed birds and big chunks of rock were lined along the mantelpiece. The hairy head of a bull buffalo hung over it. More stuffed animal heads were mounted around on the walls. A whole bear was set up in one corner, rearing on its hind legs, with forelegs upraised and its jaws gaping open to show long white fangs. It reminded him of Jasper attacking in the darkness. He wondered if the teeth were real.

No one came to investigate the sounding of the bell. The smell of cooking was strong. It stirred impatience in him. It didn't seem to be coming from the hallway at the back of the room. He turned toward the wide glass-paneled doors at his right. They were curtained, but slightly opened. He walked over cautiously and looked in.

The room was bright and cheery. Sunlight streamed sharply through big glass windows onto a long table with chairs ranked down either side. The muslin tablecloth was crisp snowy white. Each place was set with a knife and fork, a turned-over plate, a cup upside down in a saucer, a drinking glass, and a cloth napkin. The polished tableware and glasses sparkled in the sun's rays. The cloth all looked spotlessly-clean, the delft thoroughly scrubbed.

He'd been in a dining room as elegant as this before in his life. But that was a long time ago, when he'd been an artilleryman gone into some town to raise a little hell between battles. That had been someone else. Hawkins could recall the memories, but he had no feeling of their belonging to *him*. This bright, clean, hushed room he faced awed him. It frightened him.

The well-dressed man had pulled off his overcoat and was hanging it on a peg tree in the corner. He put his hat over the peg and started for a place at the table. As he turned, he saw Hawkins.

Their eyes met. And Hawkins started to pull back. But the man smiled and called, "Good morning."

Hawkins nodded in automatic response.

"Come on in," the man said. "We're both a little

early, but there's no harm in it."

Hesitantly, Hawkins stepped through the doorway. He was miserably aware of the ragged scrub of beard and the dirt he hadn't had a chance to wash off. Despite the hunger, he had a strong urge to turn and run.

It's getting worse, he thought. The world was getting less real and more fearsome. It was like being feverish, like getting sicker and sicker every day. Only there wasn't any fever. He brushed his hand across his face as if he felt his skin to be sure of it.

Once, back before he'd been into battle, one of the soldiers had told him running away never solved being afraid, but just made it worse. The more you run, the more you've *got* to run. He told himself he'd never escape the nightmares if he kept running from the things that were real.

With taut effort, he walked into the room.

Something crashed. Glass shattered. A woman's gasping scream knifed through the morning stillness.

Wheeling, Hawkins saw her. She'd just come through a door at the back of the dining room. There was a tray tilted in her hand and a broken pitcher lying in a puddle of water at her feet. Her other hand was raised, knuckles pressed against her open mouth. Her eyes were wide in startled horror. She was staring at him.

Bolting his chair, the well-dressed man scrambled toward her. He fumbled under his coat and came out with a pocket pistol. "What's the matter!"

She didn't seem to hear. She stared at Hawkins. In a pain-filled raw whisper, she said, "You're dead!"

He understood. Suddenly calm, he answered, "No, ma'am. Are you Jacob Hawkins' wife?"

There was no change in her face, but she nodded slightly.

The well-dressed man looked toward Hawkins. "What is this? What's the matter?"

"I ain't Jake," Hawkins said. "I'm his brother. I'm Eben."

She shook her head in denial. "Eben's dead, too. Jake told me."

"No, ma'am, I ain't dead." He was walking toward her. She drew the hand away from her mouth and held it out as if to stop him.

He stopped. "Jake might of thought I was dead, but I ain't."

Tentatively she stretched out her fingers and touched his coat sleeve. It seemed to reassure her. The fear in her eyes flickered and weakened. "You're not Jake?"

"I'm Eben," he said again.

She seemed to go limp, almost to fall. He reached to grab her. The well-dressed man's hands caught her arms. With a shake of her head, she blinked open her eyes. She straightened, pulling away from the hands, and stood looking at Hawkins. The fear was gone, but her face was still sickly pale.

"I—I'm terribly sorry," she stammered, not quite meeting his eyes. "You look so much like Jake's—like Jake."

*Like Jake's corpse fresh up from the grave,* he wondered. He should have known she'd see the likeness. He told himself he should have waited and got cleaned up first, not come in here looking like this.

She glanced at the broken pitcher, then faced him. She was gathering her composure. There was more color in her cheeks. She shaped her mouth into a smile. "I'm glad you've come, Eben Hawkins. We've got so much to talk about. Will you—you'll have breakfast here, won't you? We can talk afterward."

38

He nodded.

"It'll just be a little while. I've got work." She gestured toward the broken pitcher. "Got to clean up this mess."

"Are you sure you're all right, Missus Hawkins?" the well-dressed man asked.

She turned her smile to him and nodded. Then she looked to Hawkins again. "I hope you'll be staying in Garrison awhile, Mister Hawkins."

That sounded all wrong. He couldn't recall any part of his life when people had called him *Mister* Hawkins. It seemed almost as if the word made some kind of demand on him. It made him feel uncomfortable.

"Don't call me that, ma'am," he said.

"What?"

*"Mister* Hawkins. It don't sound right."

"May I call you Eben?"

That didn't sound right either. It was strange and familiar both at once. And it brought back memories that belonged to a boy named Eben who'd been happy and sure of himself, who'd worked on the farm and ranged in the woods and who'd never understood really being hungry.

He told himself that it was his name. By right. It was his, the same as those memories were. Slowly, he said, "Yes'm, Eben."

"And you'll call me Alice."

He nodded again.

As she went back into the kitchen, the well dressed man spoke to him. "So you're Jake's brother?"

He made no answer.

"It's good you've come. This has been terribly hard for her. She's a fine girl. So young, though, to be alone in the world."

He only half-heard the man's voice, and he paid no attention to it. Without looking at them, he was uncomfortably aware of the other people who'd come into the dining room. He wished he could take his meal somewhere else. Alone.

Turning his back on the man, he pulled out a chair at the end of the table and seated himself. He waited silently, his eyes fixed on the plate in front of him.

He repeated the name over in his mind, and over again. He studied on it, trying to make it fit. *Eben Hawkins.* It was his name. All of it. He wasn't just a piece of a man with a piece of a name. He wasn't just *Hawkins,* not even with a number strung after it. There wasn't any number now, but a whole name.

He was Eben Hawkins—the same Eben whose boyhood memories he had in his head. Concentrating, he tried to convince himself of that.

# CHAPTER 4

PEOPLE KEPT COMING IN UNTIL THERE WERE ABOUT A dozen of them at the long table. Alice Hawkins hurried back and forth to the kitchen, bringing out dishes of food. There were five kinds of meat, game, and fowl. There were eggs, vegetables, buckwheat cakes, and hot biscuits. There were preserved fruits, as well as honey and molasses, and other things. It was food enough for way more than a dozen people. And it was all good.

Eben Hawkins fought to keep himself from gulping at it, eating too fast and too much. He told himself there'd be more the next time he wanted it. As long as he had money, there'd be food for the buying. But the feeling was in him that he *had* to eat all he could while he had the chance, and it drove him. He stopped himself by leaving the dining room abruptly.

Outside, he headed for the barbershop. The barber was just unlocking the door when he got there. He had to wait for the fire to be built up and water heated. He sat thumbing through old papers, studying curiously on the things in them and ignoring the barber's attempts to converse.

Like the food, the hot bath seemed too much of a rare luxury to be given up once he had it. He loafed in the tub and almost fell asleep. Finally he forced himself to give it up. The clean drawers and fresh blue flannel shirt from his kit felt good against scrubbed skin.

He considered the image that gazed back at him from the barber's big wall mirror. It looked a damnsight more respectable than the one he'd seen when he came in, but it was still too lean, too darkly sullen and wary. The eyes were too uncertain. It didn't look the way he felt *Eben Hawkins* should. Eben would have smiled. He tried it, but the expression looked as wrong as the name felt. It didn't fit the face at all.

He paid the barber and headed back to the lodging house.

The dining room was empty and the table cleared of dirty dishes. He made himself rap at the kitchen door.

Alice opened it. She smiled at him, obviously approving the change in his appearance. "I was afraid you weren't coming back."

"I want to know about Jake," he said.

The smile weakened. The sorrow of memories flickered in her eyes. "I'll be through here in a few minutes. We can talk. Will you wait? You can sit in the lobby."

"I'd sooner wait outside."

41

"It's cold out."

"No, ma'am. I'd sooner wait outside..

"All right," she said. "I'll be along in a minute."

He went out the front door. The chairs on the gallery were empty. He chose one in the shadows and settled into it. Leaning back, he watched the people who ambled along the street. A wagon clattered past and stopped at the hardware store. A couple of cowboy-dressed men on small, wiry ponies, came by at a gallop. He looked close at them, but neither one was Cully. He couldn't figure why he felt disappointed at that.

It seemed like a long time before Alice finally came out. He remembered to stand up until she'd seated herself in the chair next to his. Then he sat down again with his hat in his lap. He looked at the ragged hole Jasper's shot had torn in the brim. That had been awful close.

"What did Jake die of?" he asked.

She was so slow of answering that he looked at her. And for the first time he *saw* her.

Her eyes were a brown edging on gold, set deep in a slender fine-boned face. They were large, with a wistful look to them, as if they saw dreams that were too far away to reach. Hair a darker brown than the eyes was too fine to stay put in the ribbon that bound it at the back of her neck. Wisps of it fluffed out and curled around her face. It was a young face, but there was no youthful joy in it. She looked like a lost child.

The dress she wore was severe black, and so was the shawl she held over her shoulders. He realized she was in mourning for Jake. He'd been thinking all along about how he'd lost his brother. Now it occurred to him that she'd lost her husband. She might feel as hard-struck by it as he did. And he'd come here like this,

42

abruptly calling up all the saddest memories for her.

She seemed to shiver. He thought it might be because of the memories, but he asked, "Are you cold?"

"A little." She tried to smile.

"Come on, we'll go inside." He rose, gesturing, and remembered to open the door for her.

The lobby was still empty, but a small fire had been laid on the hearth. It made a little ring of warmth. They sat down together on the sofa nearest it. After a moment, she let the shawl fall loose on her shoulders.

The dress was severe and very plain, but it was fitted above the waist. He could see the shape of her breasts under it. Stirred and embarrassed, he looked away from her.

As if she'd forgotten his question, she said, "Jake thought you'd been killed in the war. What happened to you, Eben?"

He ran his fingers through his hair. He could feel the welt of a scar on his scalp. He muttered, "I got hurt. Captured."

"Jake told me you were just a boy. He'd get awfully mad when he talked about it. He said you were too young to have gone to war."

"Maybe I was. I didn't figure that, though. I felt like a growed man back then."

"How old were you?"

"'Bout fifteen, I reckon. Maybe some over it. That was early in 'sixty-three."

Surprised, she asked, "The Army took you that young?"

He nodded. "Out in the field sometimes they got right shorthanded. I was old enough to swab out a gun and tar an axle. Captain told me if I'd say I was eighteen, he'd muster me in. We both knew it for a lie, but it didn't

43

matter none."

"Tell me about it."

He looked sideways at her, wondering why she'd want to know. There was something strange in her face, almost a desperation. It occurred to him that she wanted to keep him talking so he wouldn't ask her questions and make her go through memories that hurt. It wasn't fair, he thought. He had memories that hurt, too. But he did as her eyes asked.

"Jake went off and 'listed right after the war begun. Left me home with our folks. Everything went along all right for a while, but then the fever come into our mountains. Both our folks died of it. I couldn't see no reason to stay put then, so I packed out to hunt for Jake. I come on to the Army, in the field. This horse artillery outfit, some of the men shared food with me. They were real decent to me, so I hung around awhile, helping with the horses and things like that. They'd been in a lot of fighting. Needed men. Had more fighting ahead of 'em, too. So the captain 'listed me. I soldiered all that summer. Then we got into this battle and something went wrong. I never got straight was it that our gun got hit, or just blew up. Whatever it was, it got me."

He ran his hand into his hair, touching the scar again. "I didn't know nothing more. Not for a long time. Started to get my sense back, it was into winter and I was on Belle Island."

"A prisoner? You were captured and didn't even know about it?"

That was a piece of what worried him. There were black unknown weeks, and the men had told him that during them he'd walked around and talked like he had his sense about him.

"Yes'm," he muttered, hoping she wouldn't ask him

any more.

She looked at him as if she pitied him. He didn't want that. He said, "After a time I ran away."

She smiled as if that came as a relief to her. Then she said, "You should have gone home, or written your neighbors, or something. After the war, Jake went back to look for you. That was when he heard you'd been killed."

"Yes'm. I got back there, and they told me he'd been and gone. Said he'd sold the land and headed out here to build the railroad. I set out to find him."

"But that was eight years ago!"

He nodded. There'd been delays. The long months at Andersonville—they'd been shipped there from Belle Island—then the Rebs had got worried by Sherman's invasion and sent them to Blackshear. From there, they'd been moved again toward Savannah. It wasn't until then that he'd managed to escape. After that there'd been the hiding and hunting for Union lines—the long dark, feverish times in the swamps—then the hospital. Finally, so much later, the trip back to Kentucky. But by then Jake had already gone. And when he'd set out to follow, he'd only gotten as far as Cairo, Illinois. That was where he'd done the killing and been arrested. And then there'd been over seven years in the penitentiary.

He said, "I had some troubles following after him."

"But you kept looking. All these years you kept looking for him. You must have been very close to each other."

"I wanted real bad to find him."

The wistful sorrow was in her face. She whispered, "I loved him very much, too."

She was looking at him as if there were a tie of some

kind between them. Something that would obligate him to her. He felt an urge to explain that it wasn't just brother-love that had sent him hunting Jake after all these years. It was fear. Now, with Jake dead, he felt worse afraid than ever.

He didn't want this woman looking to him for anything. There was nothing he could give her.

Her smile was very small and very forced. Her chin quivered slightly. As she drew a deep breath, he knew she was gathering her courage. He'd answered her questions, and now she was preparing herself to answer his.

He could tell that it would pain her to talk about Jake's death. It wasn't something he *had* to know, he told himself. Knowing wouldn't bring Jake back. It wouldn't solve *his* problems. He said, "You don't have to tell me."

"I want to." Her eyes were moist, but steady. She seemed to be drawing tighter the bond that she thought was between them. He almost squirmed under her gaze. He wanted to run away.

"I'm from Chicago. My whole family—the fire—" she began, but she faltered. She looked at him as if she thought he'd understand.

But he didn't know what she meant at all. He muttered, "The fire?"

She seemed surprised. "Two years ago, when the city burned. You didn't know about that?"

"No'm."

Frowning slightly in puzzlement, she studied him. But her own memories had hold of her. In a moment she returned to them. "My whole family died in the fire. I was alone—terribly alone. An agent found work for me as a waitress in a restaurant in Cheyenne City. That's

46

where I met Jake. He started coming in every day and talking to me. After a while, we began walking out together."

The sadness and happiness in her were mixed in a pain so strong that he could feel it himself. He stared at the hearth, unable to look directly at her. He wished he could escape her. He wished to hell he could help her somehow.

"Last spring he filed on land in Clear Creek Valley and we were married," she continued. "He built a cabin and we moved in. It was very lovely. Even in the winter it would have been—it's sheltered up there, and the weather's not nearly so hard as—it—it's—"

He glanced sideways at her. "You don't have to tell me."

She caught her breath and went on as if she hadn't heard him. "Jake's horse came back. I found him in the rocks. He was dead—he—they said he must have been thrown—dragged by a stirrup—the way his—he'd been battered. He—it—" Choking on the words, she pressed her face into her hands.

He couldn't look at her. There was nothing he could say. He struggled to find something, but he couldn't. He stared at the hearth in misery.

"I'm sorry," she said softly. She caught a deep sob of breath, then shook her head as if she could pull away from the painful memories. Taking another breath, she steadied herself and asked, "What are you going to do now, Eben?"

"I don't know."

"There's work around here. The ranchers are hiring men now. And there's the railroad," she said hopefully. "You could stay here."

"No'm," he said it so faintly that she might not have

heard it. She didn't seem to.

"You could homestead the way Jake did. There's lots of good land to be had for the filing fee and the working of it."

"Homestead?" He knew the word, but not the way she seemed to mean it.

"Under the Homestead Act. Don't you know about that?"

He shook his head.

She eyed him with puzzled curiosity. "You can claim a hundred and sixty acres, anywhere the land's been opened for it. You just pay a ten-dollar filing fee and the register's charges."

"That's all? Anybody can do it?"

"Anybody except Confederates. You have to build a house and raise crops for five years, and then you get full title to the land. That's all."

It sounded like a real bargain, he thought. Only it wasn't for him. He couldn't take on anything like owning land.

But another thought was stirring in him. He asked, "Jake filed on his land last year?"

She nodded.

"But you ain't living on it now. Have you got somebody working it for you?"

"I had to give it up. After Jake died, the stock all disappeared. The cabin burned down. There wasn't any way I—I couldn't rebuild and work it by myself. I couldn't—"

"Have you already give it up, or could you keep it if you got another house built and a crop in this spring?"

"I don't know. I haven't done anything. I suppose it would be up to the land agent in Cheyenne. But—but I can't."

"*I* could." The excitement twisted inside him. He got to his feet and walked over to the fireplace. Through the sense of confusion, he clung to one thought that was sharp and clear. This was a thing he could do. And he had to do something—for himself—for her.

He gazed into the flames as he spoke. "We were farm folk back in Kentucky. Mountain country like this. It shouldn't be too different out here, should it? I might not could build you any fancy house, but I could put up a cabin like our folks lived in 'fore they built their house. I could put in a crop. If that's all that had to be done, I could do it."

"Would you, Eben?"

He heard the sudden joy in her voice, and it pleased him. The obligation he was offering to take on was frightening, but the sense of pleasure and of hope was far stronger.

"Yes'm," he said.

She rose and came toward him. Reaching out, she caught his hands in hers. He faced her, feeling the warmth of her grip. She was smiling. A very real smile.

"It meant so much to Jake. To me. We'll be partners in it, Eben."

He shied back at that thought. "No, ma'am, I'll work for you. I'll hire against what I can profit you."

"But, Eben—"

"No, ma'am," he repeated firmly. "You've got to let me do it my own way. You've got to—got to not mind me if I'm strange sometimes."

Her eyes widened in question. But her hands held to his. "All right, Eben."

He led her back to the sofa and seated her. "You're going to have to tell me a lot of things. About the land and this homestead business. And we'll need tools and things, I s'pose. You got anything left from the old place?"

"Not much. Mostly just Jake's personal belongings. So much was burned . . ." She paused, the happiness suddenly gone from her face. "Eben, I think—I think someone set fire to our cabin and ran off our stock on purpose. I think Jake was murdered."

"You'd better tell me about that, too."

As she talked, she took his hand again. She clung to it and told him about a sheltered valley where the wild grasses grew long and lush in the summer, and the winters were gentle without the heavy drifts and bitter winds that came to so much of this land.

A rancher had begun wintering his stock in the valley before it was opened to homesteaders. When the first settlers had gone in, the cattleman had complained, then threatened them. After that things had begun to happen. Stock disappeared and fires started mysteriously. One by one those first settlers had given up and gone.

Jake's holding had been the best quarter section in the valley. He'd been determined to keep it. He'd shrugged off threats, reassuring his wife that there was no real danger. But then the mules had both died suddenly. Poisoned, he'd thought. Cattle had stampeded into the valley and over his crops. He'd thought they were driven in.

He'd tried complaining to the law. But there wasn't law enough in this wild country to offer protection. And since he had no proof that anything had been done intentionally, he'd been unable to get action of any kind.

He'd refused to give up, though. Then one December day he'd ridden out and hadn't come back.

Alice had found the mangled body.

There were people who agreed with her that Jake

50

might have been murdered, but again there was no proof. The doctor who examined the body admitted that Jake might have been beaten to death, but he'd said it looked more like he'd been dragged by a stirrup. That was the official decision.

The stock that had disappeared while Alice was in town might have strayed of its own accord. The fire that destroyed the cabin might have sprung up in the mysterious natural way that fires sometimes did. There was no proof —no real evidence at all—that anyone had caused any of the troubles.

Folks sympathized with the widow, but when she talked about trying to keep the farm, they told her it was hopeless. No one had succeeded in homesteading in Clear Creek Valley. No one ever would.

Alone, she'd accepted that decision. Then Eben's sudden appearance and his offer to work the land had raised her hopes. But as she told him the things she believed, the doubts stirred in her.

Looking into his face, clinging to his hand, she said, "I'm afraid. If you try to rebuild the farm, they may hurt you, too. They may even try to kill you."

He studied her eyes. Lonely, pleading eyes. For a brief time he'd seen confidence and dreams in them. Now all of that was gone. He saw only her fear and hopelessness.

The world had bucked and spun suddenly, shifting his position in it. He'd come here feeling lost and helpless himself. He'd been afraid to try facing a world that had moved years past him. He'd hoped to find Jake and to hang on to him for protection and guidance. He'd *needed* Jake.

Abruptly all that had changed. Jake was dead. He was alone. And Jake's widow was turning to him, looking to *him* for the help that she needed.

She gripped his hand and looked at him with those wistful eyes. She was prepared to give him her trust. She needed him just as much as ever he'd felt he needed Jake.

But she said, "I couldn't let you do something dangerous—get hurt—on my account."

He shook his head. The possibility of physical danger didn't frighten him. He'd known that often enough in the past He wanted his life, but he didn't count it too valuable to risk—especially not the way things were—not when the plans and hopes he'd had were all buried with his brother's corpse. It was the obligation—the faith and trust she was willing to give—that scared hell out of him.

But no matter how strong the urge to run might be, he *couldn't* back up and quit on her.

"No, ma'am," he said. "I'm gonna do it."

"But—"

"I *got* to do it."

There was puzzlement in her gaze. She asked, "It's important to you, Eben?"

"Yes'm."

"But you hardly know me."

"I know you enough," he muttered softly. He knew the sense of loss and unreachable dreams that was in her. He understood them too damned well. There was a sameness they shared deep down. He knew that. And he had a feeling that if he could do this for her—if he could salvage some part of her dreams—he could do as much for himself. To fail her would be to lose everything.

"I'll do it," he said again. Drawing a deep breath, he put his thoughts to the immediate problems. "We'll need money for supplies and tools and seed to start. I got some, but it won't go far for stuff like that."

"I can't take your money, Eben."

"Dammit, woman, *I'll* do this! You hear me?" He startled her. And himself as well.

For an instant she drew back. Then she smiled. The trust in her eyes was complete. Obediently, she said, "Yes, Eben."

He found himself grinning at her. "All right. First I reckon I'll need an ax . . ."

# CHAPTER 5

THE HORSE THE STABLEMAN SOLD HIM HAD A MEAN streak in it. He could tell that before he tried mounting. It was a wiry, shaggy little animal with a fierce rolling eye. As he started for a stirrup, it snorted, breath pluming in the chill morning air, and turned that white-rimmed eye on him. When it lowered its head and flattened its ears, he knew it was thinking evil thoughts.

Apprehensive, he shortened the reins and swung briskly on board. The horse tried to pitch him off before he could settle. But artillery horses hadn't been easy to sit either. He discovered that his body remembered better than his mind did. His hands and legs responded. He caught balance in the deep saddle, thighs snug to it. His hands hauled back, jerking up the animal's head.

It was an ornery horse but not a wild one. After a moment of struggling, it came resentfully under his control. He gigged it, feeling its answer to the reins, then turned it onto the road up into the mountains. It tested him a couple more times for weakness, then gave up and settled into an easy rocking lope at his command.

The directions Alice had given him were simple

enough. Most of the way he could follow the ranch road. A few landmarks would guide him to a bluff. From there, he'd be able to see what was left of the cabin in the valley and pick his way down to it.

The wheel ruts crossed open land and began to climb sharply, twisting into the forest. The morning mists still hung in the shadows. He shivered as he rode into them, despite the blanket-lined canvas shortcoat he wore. That had been Jake's. So was the Henry repeating rifle he had slung on his back.

Alice had shown him the things she'd salvaged from the farm and stored away. Mostly they were just Jake's personal belongings. She'd wanted him to take whatever he could use. It had seemed wrong, but she'd insisted and he'd given in.

The clothes were generally too big for him, but he'd accepted a few things like the shortcoat. And the guns. The Henry rifle was a beautiful thing. He'd seen a few of them in the war. Sometimes soldiers saved their pay and outfitted themselves with the repeaters. He'd thought to win one in a card game once, but luck had turned on him and he'd lost two dollars instead.

The handgun was a Colt's patent five-shot pocket pistol with a four-inch barrel. It fit neatly into one pocket of the shortcoat. The box of paper cartridges for it was in the other. He hoped he wouldn't have need of it, though. He'd never handled pistols much. He'd grown up carrying a squirrel rifle and a skinning knife. He put a lot more faith in the Henry and the sheath knife he carried than in the little revolver.

The slanting sunlight made shadows dance among the trees. He watched them, thinking if he could spot any game, he'd try his hand with the rifle. It had been a hell of a long time. He wondered if that skill would come back, the way handling a horse had.

Something was moving in the woods. Halting, he unslung the rifle. He had his sights set on a patch of dun hide and was about to fire when he realized it was a cow. One of those gangling long-horned Texas cattle like he'd seen in the stock pens at Omaha.

With a grunt of disgust at himself, he lowered the gun. He'd be off to a fine start with the ranchers around here if he began by shooting their beeves. Gathering rein, he decided he'd leave off with notions of hunting until he'd learned his way around better. And then he'd make sure of what he had his sights on before he pulled the trigger.

The next time he glimpsed something moving, he just looked. It turned out to be a good-sized mule buck. With a pang of regret, he watched its rump disappear among the trees.

The ride up was a fair distance. He was saddle-weary and aching in the hip joints when he finally reached the bluff Alice had described. He slid off the horse and stretched to unkink. The air up here was really fresh, without a trace of man-scents in it. He took a deep breath, enjoying it.

The valley that spread out in front of him was a wide-bottomed basin. Across it a ridge of snowy peaks cut sharply into the midafternoon sky. Forests on the slopes reached long fingers down into the bottom land. Patches of snow lay between them, and runlets of water hurried toward the stream that meandered the length of the valley.

There were ragged outcrops of rock thrust up in places along the slopes. Some looked as sharp as fangs, some flat-faced and bare. This country had a rough wildness about it. Somehow the mountains seemed younger and less stolid than those back in Kentucky.

When he'd been a boy, he'd loved the Kentucky mountains. But he knew he couldn't go back to them now. He'd have been out of place in that set and settled land. It had belonged to a different life—a life he knew he'd never be able to return to.

But these raw, wild mountains had no memories. They were a fresh new land. They were waiting—for him? As he stood on the bluff looking across the valley, he felt as if he'd almost reached some goal. Just a few more steps, he felt, and he'd be within sight of it.

He swallowed at the rising sense of excitement. He *wanted* this land. But he was afraid of wanting things. He'd been disappointed too damned deeply before.

Moving slowly, cautious of his own emotions, he stepped to the saddle and started the horse downward, toward the rubble of charred logs he'd spotted.

Jake's quarter section was only a small corner of the valley. The cabin had been built in the lee of a rough-faced rock scarp, with the fields and open bottom land stretching out in front of it. The cover of snow on the ground now was thin enough that Eben could trace out the earth that had been broken by the plow.

He found the lower location markers easily enough. Alice had said the upper one was high on the jagged face of the rock. A spring rose up there, spilling its overflow through a deep cut in the rocks into the valley. It wandered past the cabin and across Jake's fields to join Clear Creek. The springhead was within the boundaries.

Studying the rocky face from below, Eben decided a horse couldn't possibly climb it. He'd have to clamber up afoot. It'd be a job of work. And he was bone-weary already. He'd set up his camp for the night now, and do the climbing tomorrow.

Stretching his paulin from a part of the ruined cabin, he made a lean-to of sorts. He spitted meat from his supplies over a small fire at one end. Then he set about gathering boughs to make a soft pad between his blanket and the frosty ground.

By the time he'd finished eating and was ready to bed down, the lean-to was filled with warmth from the fire. It was a snug camp, he thought as he banked the fire to keep the coals. A real good camp in a fine place. He rolled himself in the blanket and dropped quickly into sleep.

Suddenly it was morning. He'd slept through the night without troubling dreams. As he fixed breakfast, he pondered over that. It seemed as if all his life he'd slept uneasy. He couldn't recall a time when he'd wakened so sharp or felt so fresh as he did this morning. His bones still had an aching recollection of the ride up, but there was none of the dull eternal weariness he was so familiar with.

He spent a good part of the day exploring. Climbing the rocks, he found the location marker on a shallow ledge. Stretching out, belly down, on the ledge, he looked across the farmland. The hobbled horse had managed to drift a fair ways. Nosing at the snow, it seemed to be turning up plenty enough to eat.

There wouldn't be snow much longer, he thought as he felt the warmth of the sun on his back. The runoff streams were already beginning to flood. Melted snow added to the stream from Jake's spring. It filled the natural sluice with a wild, tumbling current that sang in his ears.

Half-drowsing, he made pictures in his mind—the cabin rebuilt, the fields green toward harvest, a milch cow browsing in the wild grass—maybe more than one if there was a market for the butter. There'd be hogs, of course, and a smokehouse—probably over yonder where the wind wouldn't send smoke back toward the cabin. And maybe a still tucked up in these rocks somewheres. In country like this there shouldn't be anybody to stop a man making enough corn for his own use without he had to pay up a mess of taxes on it. The water was sure pure and sweet enough. That spring of Jake's ran as fine water as he'd ever tasted.

With a thin sense of envy, he wondered how it had been for Jake, living up here with Alice. Likely damn fine, he thought.

He shook his head, shaking away the sleep that had been trying to catch hold of him. There was work to be done. He got to his feet and scanned the far slopes. The things moving along the edges of the wood were mostly cattle, he reckoned. But there was game, too. He'd found sign enough of deer and rabbits and birds. Be a good idea to set a few snares. And he could sure portion himself out some time for hunting with that repeating rifle.

As he scrambled down the scarp, he thought over the experimenting he'd done with the rifle that morning. He'd been able to place his shots well enough, once he got the feel of it. But he hadn't the quickness he thought he could remember from when he was a boy. Maybe that'd come back with time and some practice, he told himself. Maybe a lot of things would come back to him in time.

When he began to clear away the rubble, he found that Jake had set good-sized stones into the earth as supports for beams and had put down a punch floor. It had hardly been touched by the fire. And several of the logs were barely charred, not burned bad enough that he couldn't use them again. He'd need plenty more, though.

He was walking through the nearest stand of timber, studying over trees that would serve, when he spotted the red cow. It was fair close to him, and it didn't shy away like the other ones he'd come near. It just stood there, working its jaw and watching him with wide, mild eyes. It didn't have the shape of those Texas cattle either. Its legs were shorter, its build heavier. He thought it was the kind called a Devon.

A yoke ox turned out to range, he wondered. He'd heard folks didn't work cattle so much as they used to. Lots of steers broke to work were being fattened and sold for beef. He'd seen a bunch of them in the stock pens at Omaha. It seemed wasteful. He grinned slightly at his own thoughts and began to move toward the steer.

It stood a moment eying him before it backed off. But it didn't bolt. Turning, it watched curiously as he tried again. He'd almost reached it before it backed off this time.

Footing it quickly to his camp, he collected a handful of the grain he'd brought along for his horse. With that, he managed to work in closer. Finally the steer reached out a long tongue and licked it off his outstretched palm.

He slid his fingers under its chin and scratched. This was a tame old ox all right. It stretched out its neck in enjoyment. The brand burned onto its hide said it belonged to somebody, but to hell with that. Once he got his trees felled, the logs would have to be sledded over to the cabin site. An ox would be a lot better for the job than that ornery little mountain pony. When he'd finished, he'd turn the steer loose again, no harm done.

Slipping his belt around its neck, he tugged. It

59

followed him back to his camp without protest. He gave it more grain, picketed it, and got on with hunting timber.

The first day of swinging an ax put a sore aching into his back and shoulders. He quit for the day before it made raw meat of his hands. He paced himself carefully, trying to judge his limits, and slowly, he was able to extend them.

The ox proved just as useful as he'd hoped. It accepted the yoke he ax-whittled for it as if it were eager to be working again. He wondered if an animal could get lonely and bored to hell by itself, the same way a man could. The ox sure seemed happy with his company.

He felt a mite shameful of putting crude walls of untrimmed logs on the fine foundations Jake had laid. But the important thing was getting a cabin of some kind completed and crops in. Spring was coming on fast. It'd soon be time to get the earth broken. He had hopes of having the walls up by then. He could throw on a crude roof of brush and sod over poles for the summer, and worry about planks and shakes later.

As he worked at the walls, he studied on the problems of planting. He'd come up to the valley with just the tools and supplies he could pack onto his saddle. He'd concentrated on getting the cabin started, figuring he could make a trip back for a plow and seed and such if it worked out that he'd need them.

It looked like everything was going to work out fine. There hadn't been a trace of trouble. He'd glimpsed a couple of hunters in the distance, but he hadn't seen any other signs of men in all the time he'd been here.

He didn't *want* to go into town. He liked it here—liked it alone. And he resented the idea of taking time away from the work he had planned. But he'd have to get tools. And he owed it to Alice to report how he was progressing. He had a feeling he'd already put that off a lot longer than he should have.

Just as a precaution, he cached away his gear as well as his supplies. He had to turn the ox loose, but he had hopes of being able to find it again. It'd be a sight better in front of a plow than the mountain pony would. And after all, he argued himself, he wasn't costing anyone anything or doing the animal any harm by working it.

Reluctance dragged at him as he mounted up to head for Garrison. But there was nothing to be gained by stalling off a chore, just because he didn't fancy it.

It was coming twilight when he reached the town. And his mood was growing darker, too. He hated the nearness of the buildings with their looming wall-like fronts. He hated the man-scents in the air, and the memories they stirred. Feeling vaguely angry, he trotted the horse along the street.

Somebody sang out a greeting. It took him a moment to realize it was aimed at him. He looked coldly toward the man who'd called, wondering who the hell he was. Not anybody he knew. His brother's widow was the only person he knew in this town, unless he counted that brief introduction to the folks who ran the lodging house. Now he wasn't even sure he recalled their name right. Carson, he thought. Something like that.

As he drew rein in front of the lodging house, another stranger called to him. Smiling real friendly, the man tried up and asked him wasn't he Eben Hawkins.

He made no reply. He ignored the man as he stepped down from the saddle and loosened the girth. He couldn't shut out the voice, though.

"I'm Amos Beasley. Run the hardware store," the

61

man said. "Heard you'd took up the widow Hawkins' land for her. Real glad to hear it. You getting along all right out there?"

Eben turned and looked at him narrowly.

"Anything you need out there, just stop by my place. It's right up the road," he continued, hooking a thumb in the direction of his store.

"You want to sell me something," Eben grunted, remembering the way the sutlers had smiled when they offered to sell shoddy to the soldiers for fine fancy prices.

"Selling things is my business," Beasley said, still smiling cheerily. "Anything that little widow's needing from my stock, I can make her terms for it. You understand?"

Eben figured he did. This man felt guilty about the way Alice had almost lost her land without anyone to help her. He hadn't turned a hand for her then, but now he'd let out a few dollars worth of goods on credit if she wanted. He'd make his profit if he got paid, and if he didn't he'd count it charity and feel real proud of himself.

Something of Eben's thoughts must have shown in his face. The man's smile faded. He said, "I mean it, Hawkins. If you can keep a hold in that valley, you won't just be helping the widow. You'll be helping this whole town."

Eben didn't want to help the whole town. Eying Beasley warily, he asked, "How's that?"

"All of Clear Creek Valley has been opened to homestead, but so far there ain't a single settler been able to hang on there. If you do it, others'll follow you. A lot of folk will move in up there. And they'll trade here in Garrison. It'll profit us all."

"Won't profit me none," he grumbled, turning away from the man. He didn't want to help their town, and he damned well didn't want other folk in the valley.

He strode up the lodging house steps, his heels hammering hard on them The bell jangled frantically as he jerked open the door. He slammed it behind him.

The woman who came scurrying into the lobby was Mrs. Carson, or whatever her name was. She was frowning at the racket he'd made, but as she recognized him, she smiled. She greeted him as if he were kinfolk,

Squirming away from her welcome, he asked gruffly for Alice.

"She's finished her work for the day. I think she went up to her room," the woman told him. "Will you be staying for the night? I'll fix a bed for you."

"No."

She gave him a motherly smile. "Don't worry. Things are slow right now. I'll fix you a bed, no charge."

He didn't want a bed. Not bothering to answer, he pushed past her and tromped up the stairs.

Alice's room was at the end of the hallway, to the back. He rapped sharply at the door.

It opened. She stood there just looking at him for an instant. Then, suddenly, tears streaked her face. She jerked up her hands, covering them. Her whole body shook with the violence of her crying.

He thought he must have done something wrong. Something godawful wrong to have upset her that way.

The confusion twisted in him. He didn't understand her. He was overwhelmed with the feeling that he didn't understand anything. The time he'd spent in the valley and the things he'd done there seemed like things he'd dreamed. The smell of the lodging house, the closeness of the walls in the narrow hallway, the woman sobbing as if he'd terrified her—these were the real things. They pressed in on him, threatening to crush him.

Wheeling away from her, he hurried toward the stairs. He had to get the hell away from here.

"Eben!" she called.

He paid no mind, but rushed on down the stairs. Her voice trailed after him as if it meant to haunt him. Flinging open the door, he lunged out into the twilight.

# CHAPTER 6

THE SCENT OF THE FOREST WAS IN THE RISING BREEZE. It came down from the slopes and swept through the town, stirring the lanterns that hung in front of some of the buildings, making their shadows flicker in wild dances.

Eben halted, drawing a deep breath, trying to catch rein on himself, He heard Alice's voice again.

"Eben, please . . ." she called thinly.

He looked back. She was coming onto the gallery. The urge to run again washed through him. He choked it back, telling himself that running was no good. Whatever was wrong, he *had* to face it.

She came down the steps toward him slowly. Her voice was soft and uncertain. "Eben?"

"What'd I do?" he snapped, afraid of the answer.

"You?" She sounded puzzled. The lamplight made shining tracks of the tear streaks on her face. Her eyes were still damp. She brushed at the corner of one with the back of her wrist and looked up at him.

"Crying," he mumbled, gesturing vaguely as he hunted words. "Why?"

"Oh, Eben!" She swallowed at a sob. "I'm so glad to

see you! I was so worried—afraid you were dead!"

"Huh?"

She must have read a lot in his face. Her mouth turned in a wispy smile. It looked odd against the tearstains. "You don't understand women, do you?"

He shook his head. He didn't understand anything.

Dabbing at her eyes again, she said, "Sometimes we cry when we're happy. *Very* happy."

He couldn't make sense of it. But she wasn't mad at him, or hurt by him. Relieved, but still confused, he stood wordless, not quite meeting her gaze.

"You've been gone a long time," she said. "Tell me what's happened. What have you been doing?"

"Things," he mumbled. His voice came hoarse, almost soundless. He glanced around, feeling the looming closeness of the buildings lining the street.

As if she understood, she reached for his hand and suggested, "Let's walk awhile. Where it's quiet."

She led him away from the lodging house and out of the lantern light. Away from the stink and sounds of the town.

The sun was gone behind the western ridges, but the sky was streaked with layers of bright color. The peaks were a sharp jagged black against it. The wind rustled the woods, making small sounds that were vividly different from those in the town. These sounds took nothing from the silence.

They walked through the night shadows and the cool-scented breeze, up the wheel tracks toward the low ridge. The town was behind them, unseen.

"I been building a cabin," he said suddenly.

Her hand tightened on his. "Tell me about it."

The words were hard to find at first, but it got easier. He told her what he'd accomplished and what he planned. Then he found that he was telling her all about the valley, as if she'd never been there herself. He stopped abruptly, feeling foolish, and muttered, "It's a good place."

"A good place," she echoed.

He knew she meant it. There was a sound of dreams in her voice, as if she'd seen it in the same way he had. He thought about that as they walked on.

Beyond the little ridge, the golden sky was fading into a glowing violet-black. The first stars were shining like pinpoints poked through smoked parchment. As they reached the top of the ridge, she halted him with a tug of her hand.

"Let's rest here a minute."

It was dark. He didn't see the windfallen log until she seated herself on it. She gestured for him to sit down beside her.

"I used to come up here," she said, almost whispering. "I missed Jake so. I wanted to be alone. Away from everyone else."

"You sooner I left?" he asked, starting to rise.

"Oh, no!" She caught his hand, holding him there.

He settled again, and sat beside her in the silence, hearing her soft-drawn breath. He was aware of the warmth of her body and the woman-scent of her. Too damned aware of her womanness.

With a tinge of anger, he wondered if she might know that. Or had she forgotten that being her dead husband's brother didn't stop him of being a man, too.

She shouldn't treat him so much like family, he thought. She shouldn't be so free and at ease around him. Just because she'd been married to Jake didn't make her *his* close kin. Not in *that* way—not like he was her blood brother or a first cousin or something.

He wished to hell he hadn't had to come into town. Everything had been fine and right in the valley. Here, it was all wrong. It twisted him inside, tearing at his vitals.

"What's the matter, Eben?" she asked from the darkness.

"Nothing!"

He knew as he said it that it was too loud and harsh and sounded like a lie. But he was so damned confused. Leaning his head into his hand, he ran his fingers through his hair. He touched the welt of the scar, wondering if whatever had made that wound had cracked his skull as well. And addled his wits.

She said nothing. But he could sense that she was waiting. He could feel it driving at him. Without speaking a word, she was asking something of him. He didn't know what, though.

It occurred to him that she might be looking for a man to take Jake's place. He knew it was a hard thing for a woman to be widowed. Especially hard for a young one like Alice, with no family to look out for her. He figured her to be a couple or three years younger than he was. Just a girl. Orphaned, widowed, and alone out here in this raw, wild country with nobody at all to take care of her. Likely she was awfully lonely.

Since he was Jake's brother, she might be thinking he was like Jake. She might have a notion he'd make the same kind of husband that Jake had been. She hadn't any way to know how wrong that idea was—unless he told her.

And he couldn't do that. Even if he'd wanted to spell it all out, he didn't know words to put it into. Even in his own mind, he couldn't find a way to explain.

But he could warn her off. He considered that thought, fearful that telling her any part of it would frighten her. Maybe she'd want him to give up the farm, if she knew more about him. But he felt he had to tell her at least some of it.

"Ma'am," he started. Somehow it sounded wrong. But he couldn't think of a way to right it. He pushed on. "Ma'am, these past seven years—where I been—I been in prison."

"I thought it might have been something like that," she said softly.

"Huh?"

"Things you've said, ways you have about you. I thought of prison. Is that what's been bothering you so, Eben?" She sounded like it wasn't really very important at all.

"I killed a man."

"Are they hunting you for it?" she asked. There was concern in her voice and in the touch of her hand on his. Concern for him.

"No, ma'am. I been pardoned free."

"Then it's all past, isn't it, Eben?" She sighed with relief.

"Ain't nothing past!" The words were suddenly saying themselves to her as he listened. "There ain't nothing *past* at all. It's all mixed up together. I *know* where I am and when it is, but the feelings I get ain't right for the time and the place. They belong back there, somewhere else. The feelings of the dreams get all mixed in. I get so damned hungry, only there ain't no reason. I—I *know* what's real! Only I can't help it! Sometimes I think I ain't right in the head."

He expected her to draw away in horror from a madman and a murderer. But she held on to his hand.

Gently, she said, "It's all past, Eben."

He shook his head, though he knew she couldn't see

68

it in the darkness. Rising, he muttered, "We better go back."

She came along at his side, still holding on to his hand.

He walked in silence, struggling with his thoughts, wondering about himself and about her. She hadn't turned away, hadn't even flinched. She took what he'd said and hadn't even asked him how he'd come to kill or if he'd repented it. She seemed to accept him.

He stopped her before they reached the lights of the town. He wished he could see her face. But he didn't want light. He couldn't say what he planned if he were in the light.

Hesitant and fearful, he began, "Ma'am, I think maybe you know me now. Leastways, you know what's bad about me. But I can work a farm and I'm willing. I could keep a woman fed and a roof patched up for her. And I wouldn't come in drunk and beat her or nothing like that.

"I know it's hard for you being a widow," he went on before she could interrupt. "And maybe you're looking for a man. I s'pose it ain't always easy to find one. If you figure you can't get better than me—maybe—look, ma'am, if what you want is for me to marry you, I'll do it. If you want."

Her hand pulled away from his. He knew he'd startled her. But he couldn't tell what her answer might be. He wished to hell he could see her face.

For long, long moments, she said nothing. Then, stiffly, she answered, "That's not what I want, Eben."

She began to walk toward the town.

He followed a half a stride behind her. His hand hung at his side, feeling cold and empty without hers in it. He couldn't read his own feelings. He'd been bad scared she'd accept him. But there was no relief in the answer he'd gotten.

At the lodging house steps she paused and turned toward him. Her face was taut and solemn in the lamp glow. Huskily, she said, "I think you meant—I—I appreciate your thoughtfulness, Eben."

Whirling, she hurried up the stairs.

He watched her disappear into the building. Then he tightened the girth and stepped up onto his pony. He had a feeling he couldn't stand being in the town much longer. He couldn't go back to the valley yet, though. There was business to be tended here.

Riding into the woods, he unrolled his blanket well beyond sight of the town. For a long while he lay unsleeping. And when he finally did drowse, his dreams were troubled. He couldn't remember them, come morning, but he could still feel the ugliness of them along his spine.

He was worried about what Alice would be thinking of him now. He was sure he'd done wrong by what he'd said to her, but he didn't intend to give up the farm unless she outright ordered him to go. And she couldn't do that if he managed to avoid seeing her.

He didn't dare go to the dining room, so he bought crackers and cheese and an airtight of sweet peaches at the grocery. The food filled his belly, but it didn't much help the feeling of hunger. He went back for a piece of dried meat he could chew on like a tobacco cud. It didn't help much either, but he gnawed at it as he hurried to tend his business in town.

He used up the last of his money buying things he'd need on the farm. It wasn't nearly everything he'd thought of, but once he managed to get it all packed onto the horse, there was no space left for him. Afoot, he set out leading the shaggy pony up the ranch road.

A farmer really needed a wagon, but wagons cost money and he was out of that. Besides, the old wagon road into the valley had been abandoned and was blocked with winter windfalls. It'd take time for a man alone to clear it. He didn't have much of that to spare either. Come harvest, though, he'd *have* to have a wagon. He considered the problem as he walked. It might be once he got a crop in, he could borrow against it. But that would mean a debt—an obligation. Just the notion of it made him feel uneasy.

The problems, the thoughts of Alice, the idea that he might still have trouble with the rancher, nagged at him. A sense of apprehension drew along the back of his neck. He tried to shake free of it, but he couldn't. When he glimpsed riders up the road, he automatically ducked off into the woods.

There wasn't any reason to hide. He told himself that the feeling of danger, of being hunted, belonged back in Georgia when he'd escaped into the swamps. But he couldn't argue himself out of it. He kept hidden in the woods until the riders were well past.

Traveling afoot took time. By nightfall he was still a fair distance from the valley. With the sense of trouble gnawing at him, he made a cold camp well away from the road. He got moving again early, but even so it was far into the afternoon when he finally reached the cabin.

He was too tired and footsore to do more than dump the load off the horse. Dragging himself into the half-built cabin, he pulled off his boots and stretched out on the floor. He lay there, not exactly awake, but not asleep, gazing at the open sky above. He wished the roof was on. So damned much work to be done . . .

Something was moving outside. Suddenly alert, he

lay motionless. It was easy to tell which sounds were made by his own horse and which belonged to the valley. Those slow, dull footfalls were neither.

Cautiously he sat up and reached for the rifle. He started silently toward the doorway.

Something thudded against the wall. Whatever it was, it seemed to be at the back of the cabin. He stepped out into the twilight shadows. The earth was cold under his feet. He shivered, remembering winter on Belle Island.

At the corner of the cabin he paused. He could hear heavy breathing. The rifle trembled slightly in his hands. Jerking the lever, he edged forward.

As he stepped from cover the wide, mild eyes of the ox looked up at him. It thrust out its head to be scratched.

He shuddered with a deep sigh of relief. Grinning, he cursed the animal affectionately and rubbed it under the jaw. Then he gave it a shove and leaned back against the wall, feeling too exhausted to even walk back inside.

After a while he stirred himself to finish his chores and eat a cold meal out of a can. When at last he bedded, he dropped into a dark, restless sleep.

He wakened weary, hungry, and still footsore. Contemplating his battered boots, he recalled times he'd followed a plow barefoot. When he was a kid, he'd hated shoes, but as he grew older he'd gotten accustomed to them. After he'd been captured and the Rebs confiscated his boots, he'd damned well missed them. Especially in the icy winter on Belle Island. He'd sworn to himself then that once he got free, he'd never go without them again.

Now, he told himself, it would be foolish to put them on for no better reason than that. He didn't feel like cramming his feet into them. And they'd last him a lot longer if he did without them when he could. Hell, the days when he'd gone barefoot for lack of any choice were long past. Shoving the boots into a corner, he walked gingerly out of the cabin. The ground was chilly but not uncomfortably cold. After a few minutes, he stopped noticing it.

The fields had been broken before. They were sprouting weeds now, but they were clear of rocks and heavy roots. He marked out the corners he intended to work to, hitched the ox to the plow, and set in the first furrow.

Leaning his arms on the steer's rump, he looked back at it. Not quite as even or straight as it might have been, but not bad at all. Grinning with pride, he said aloud, "Well, old cow, we've started."

The ox switched its tail and grumbled somewhere deep inside.

"Got to turn the row," he said, straightening up and taking hold of the line again. He brushed at a fly that buzzed near his face, then leaned on the plow. "Turning's the hard part. Haw, old cow!"

The ox moved, not seeming to notice the yoke on its neck or the weight of the plow it pulled. The earth rose on the moulding board, turning in loose, loamy clods. The turn was ragged, but the furrow fairly straight.

When he stopped to grab himself a midday meal, he peeled his shirt. By early afternoon, he'd shucked his undershirt as well. The air was cool, but the sun and the work slicked his skin with sweat. He'd paused to mop at his face with a kerchief when he spotted the riders.

There were two of them, coming downvalley toward him at a hard gallop. Cowboys from the look of them.

He glanced at the cabin where he'd left the rifle, wondering if he should fetch it. But he didn't want

73

trouble if it could be avoided. There was no proof these men were planning any. They were riding in openly. Greeting them with a gun in his hand could be a poor way to start things.

They came closer, two young hard-faced men in broad-brimmed hats. They wore vests but no coats and tucked their breeches into high boots like the ones Cully'd worn. Each had a handgun in a holster on his belt and a coiled rope on his saddle.

As Eben waited, watching them, the breeze touched him, drying the sweat on his skin. He shivered at the chill.

The men drew rein sharply, side by side. Both jerked their horses back to sudden downhaunched stops. They looked at Eben, at the unfinished cabin and half-plowed field, and at the yoked ox through narrowed eyes. Silently, they studied over the farm, then turned to Eben again.

He stood impassive, waiting.

The taller one leaned an arm on his saddle horn. He worked his jaw, spat tobacco juice, and said, "You new in these parts?"

Eben nodded.

"That your cabin?"

He nodded again.

"And your horse up yonder?" The cowboy jerked his head toward the pony hobbled out to graze.

Eben gave him the same wordless answer.

"What about that steer?" He jutted his chin toward the ox. "That yours, too?"

"I'm working him," Eben said warily.

The cowboy pursed his lips as if he were speculating on something. He spat again and spoke with a sly edge to his voice. "Brand on that steer's hide says it belongs to my boss."

"I didn't say I *owned* it."

"You just sort of borrowed it?" The tall cowboy's face was solemn. His partner grinned slightly.

Eben nodded again, knowing now that he should have gone for the gun. But it was too late. The riders had edged between him and the cabin. Even if he did break and run, he couldn't get there.

Slipping the plowline from around his neck, he wiped at his face with the back of his hand. He covered a quick glance toward the nearest spit of woods. It wasn't close. To make it, he'd have to outrun a horse. Maybe a bullet.

"You got leave from Mister Starrett to borrow the loan of his beeves?" the cowboy said.

"Didn't look to me like he was using it for anything."

"Might not look to you like he's using this land either, plowboy, but he *is*. And he ain't gonna like you tearing it up that way."

"It ain't *his* land."

"Ain't it?"

"Belongs to a widow woman name of Hawkins," Eben answered, aware that it was futile.

"Mister Starrett was here before Hawkins. Been here since Hawkins. Gonna be here since you, too."

He shook his head in denial.

The cowboy studied on him, then said, "Likely Mister Starrett don't know yet that you're setting down here. He ain't mentioned it to none of us yet. If I was you, I wouldn't be here no more when he does."

"I'll be here."

"You ain't very smart, barefoot."

"Maybe not, but I'll be here."

With a mockery of a sad sigh, the cowboy said, "Well, we ain't got no orders about you yet, but we got orders to hunt up Mister Starrett's beeves. I reckon we'd better take that'n. Fetch it, will you, Joe?"

"Sure," the second man grinned, heeling his horse toward the ox. He leaned out of the saddle, knife in hand, and reached for the lines.

"Hey!" Eben started to protest. They might have the right to take the ox, but not to cut up his harness.

The first cowboy interrupted, speaking loud and firm. "And, Joe, seeing as how he took to borrow use of the steer, maybe we ought to even things up by borrowing his horse awhile."

"Like hell!" Eben snapped.

The cowboy's hand slid to his hip. He jerked it up with the revolver in it pointed at Eben. Quietly, he said, "If a feller got himself hurt trying to steal one of Mister Starrett's beeves, there wouldn't nobody make no fuss at all."

There was nothing to be gained by getting shot. Eben yielded. He stood silent, glaring, as the one named Joe slashed the ox free of the plow, then cut the pony's hobbles.

As Joe herded the horse and ox together, the other cowboy holstered his gun. He turned his mount to fall in next to Joe.

Eben started for the cabin and the rifle.

The cowboy wheeled his horse. He lunged it in front of Eben, blocking his way. Galloping past, he spun the horse on its haunches to face Eben again. The coiled rope was in his hand. He began shaking a loop into it.

Poised to run, Eben watched him uncertainly. He couldn't figure what the hell the man meant to do.

Joe gave a whooping shout of encouragement. Echoing it, the first cowboy lunged his horse again. He drove it straight toward Eben.

It came at him like an artillery team. He had to run or be ridden down. Leaping away from it, he broke toward the trees.

The cowboy was behind him. He heard the horse running and knew it could catch him before he reached cover. But it sounded like it was only pacing him. Incredulously, he thought the man only meant to chase him into the woods and leave it at that.

He was almost to the edge of the forest when the loop snapped out. It seemed as if it came from nowhere. Suddenly it was there, dropping over him. It jerked fight around his knees, pulling his legs out from under him.

He slammed face down on the ground, the breath jolted out of him.

The cowboys laughed. One of them called, "Hey, barefoot, you *like* dirt-grubbing?"

The rope was tight. He squirmed, trying to ease it so that he could stand up. But the other end was tied to the man's saddle. As he moved, the horse backed, keeping it taut. The best he could do was twist onto his side and look back at them.

Joe grinned at his partner. "Well, Pete, you throwed it. Gonna brand it now?"

"Got no fire," Pete said mournfully.

Joe nodded toward the cabin. "There's a handy heap of logs. We could start one right easy."

Moving his hand cautiously, Eben tried to reach the hilt of his sheath knife. But as his fingers touched it, Pete whooped, reining the horse back. It jerked the rope, hauling him his own length across the ground. Stones and bits of branches scraped at his ribs. He cursed thinly.

Stopping the horse, Pete hollered, "Don't mess around, plowboy! You could get hurt playin' with knives."

Eben swallowed hard at the bitter, helpless anger. He knew there wasn't a damned thing he could do.

Casually, Pete picked up his conversation with Joe. "Naw, ne'mind the fire. Boss ain't said nothing about branding up muley dirt-eating mavericks like this one."

"Reckon we ought to let him go till we find out is there a bounty for his ears?" Joe asked.

Pete nodded and nudged his horse forward, giving the rope a flick. As he felt it slacken, Eben jerked free of it. Pete drew it in and began to coil it.

"You go tend your chickens somewheres else, plowboy," he said.

Getting to his feet, Eben called back, "I'm *here*. I mean to be here a damned long time. I'll be here when your boss is gone and forgot. You can tell him that."

"You'll be here all right, boy," Joe hollered at him. "Only you'll be planted a lot deeper than them rows you been cutting." With a touch of the reins, he turned his horse toward the ox and Eben's pony. Pete swung around to fall in beside him.

As they herded the animals away, Eben ran toward the cabin. By the time he'd reached it and grabbed up the rifle, they were already past a point of the forest and turning. He could only glimpse them through the trees as he levered a shell into the chamber. With his back braced against the wall, he sighted along the barrel.

His hands were shaking. He couldn't get the gun to steady. And he could barely make out the figures moving beyond the woods.

He jerked the trigger, knowing the shot was wild and futile. The rifle bucked against his shoulder, spewing smoke and sound that echoed the anger in him but didn't relieve it. Even the thunder of a twelve-pound

Napoleon spitting shrapnel wouldn't have been violence enough to ease that anger.

Muttering curses, trembling, he looked back at the partly turned field. With both the ox and the horse gone, what the hell could he do now?

# CHAPTER 7

THERE WAS SOME SKIN SCRAPED OFF HIS BARE CHEST. A couple of the scratches were deep enough to ooze blood. He hunkered by the stream, washing at them, as he pondered the situation.

The cowboys didn't seem to have believed his fine talk about staying. They'd acted like they thought he was beaten. He had to own to himself that they'd left him feeling damned close to it. But he was calm enough now to think straight. And he was determined that nobody was running him out of the valley. The next one who came nosing around here would get greeted by the Henry rifle.

He went back to the cabin to fetch his shirt. As he pulled it on, he looked over the field. He couldn't plow without a work animal, and he hadn't the money to buy one. He couldn't count on finding another yoke ox browsing around that way either. That red steer had been a real piece of luck. It was a regular old house pet, he thought. It sure fancied a little scratching and a handful of grain.

If those cowboys let it go anywhere nearby, likely it would come right straight back here.

He grinned slightly at the idea. It was a thought worth putting some hope on. Leastways there were a lot of things to be done around the place that he could handle without a work animal. He could afford to wait a day or two for the ox. If it didn't come drifting back—well, give it a couple of days and see.

The walls of the cabin were about as high now as he could handily shift a log straight off his shoulder. He figured on a couple more across the back and three or four in front to give the roof a slope. There were side pieces to be fitted and shaped for the slant, too. Once that was done, he could start laying on poles and sod for the roof.

Glancing toward the sun, he judged he had a good four hours of daylight left. Plenty of logs cut, just waiting to be notched and hefted into place, too. Might as well fetch the ax and get started.

He went at it with an intensity that was near violence. Swinging the ax as if he meant to kill with it, he sent chips scattering wild. Sweat soaked his shirt and dripped from his face.

He stopped, finally, to wipe at the sweat and catch breath. Leaning on the ax, he scanned the valley. A damn fine place.

He and Alice had agreed on that. Remembering, he considered the thoughts he'd had that evening walking out with her. And the things he'd said. He'd been a fool offering to marry her that way. At least she hadn't been fool enough to accept him.

Likely a woman would want more from her man than just the promise that he'd work hard and not beat her. As he recalled, there'd been a damnsight more than just that and a bed to his own folks' marriage. There'd been the talk and the words that never got spoken, but passed from eye to eye in a glance. There'd been gentleness and understanding and things beyond a kid's recognizing.

That was what folks meant by *love,* he figured. From the talk he'd heard, there were plenty of people who married without it, but it seemed to be what most folks hoped for. Likely even a lonesome widow woman would hope after finding it.

Himself—he didn't understand it. He felt that he didn't understand much of anything—but most of all women and love. There weren't either in a prison. Only by the time a boy had spent a while in the army and a while more listening to the talk around a prisoner camp, he could learn a few things and begin to wonder about a hell of a lot more. And in the long, silent hours when he was supposed to be repenting his sin, he could sure come up with a lot of questions.

Alone, without Jake to help and guide him, he wondered if he'd ever find the answers to any of them.

He scrubbed his fingers into his hair, touching the scar on his scalp. He felt as if he'd been broken and thrown away in pieces. Now he had the chance to find all those pieces and fit them back together into a man again—if he could.

Well, there was one thing he was certain he could do. Even without having the learning that should have come in all the years of life he'd missed, he could damn well work and hold this farm. Nobody would stop him of that, short of killing him.

He took hold of a notched log and leaned, dragging it toward the wall. As he worked, he kept glancing at the slopes. It didn't seem likely that the cowboys would be back to check up for at least a couple of days, but he didn't mean to take any chances on it.

He decided not to sleep in the cabin that night. Packing his blanket and the rifle, he climbed to the ledge overlooking the farm and bedded there. He slept

81

slight, aware of the sounds of the night around him. When he wakened, he fixed and ate his breakfast without much thought to it. There was too much else in his mind. He didn't notice whether he was hungry or not.

The cabin grew. Measured from the floor to the top edge, the walls came even with the top of his head. That would be high enough in the back, he figured. He got a cross-log up on each side and scrambled up barefoot to secure them. He was just finishing it when he glimpsed the rider. Swinging down off the wall, he grabbed for the rifle.

The man was a good ways off yet but coming fast. Even at the distance, he was obviously a cowboy.

Eben almost started into the cabin. But instead, he wheeled and ducked behind it. The walls might make good cover, but they'd make a fine bonfire too. And it was where an attacker would expect him to hide.

He looked at the face of the scarp. There were plenty of clefts and outjuts of rock, with scatters of brush around it. Plenty of good cover. Keeping the cabin between himself and the rider, he headed for a shadowed cranny. Squeezed into it with his back against the rock and the rifle held to his chest, he waited.

The cowboy gave a holler from the distance. After a moment, he came into sight past the edge of the cabin. Swinging wide, he made a full circle around it at a lope. Then he slowed and called again. He didn't look like he expected an answer. He didn't get one.

As he moved in closer, he disappeared from Eben's sight behind the walls. Then he reappeared, seeming satisfied that the place was deserted. He ambled his horse toward the stream without more than a glance at the scarp.

The horse nosed into the water, and the cowboy slid out of the saddle. Pulling off his hat, he wiped at his face with his sleeve. Then he set the hat over the saddle horn and dropped to his knees to drink. His back was to the scarp.

Eben stepped out of cover. With rifle in his hands, but not aimed, he called, "Cully?"

The cowboy turned, half-rising. His face was wide with surprise. Frowning uncertainly at the sight of the rifle, he sank back onto his knees and held out his hands, palms up.

"*Hawk?*" he said, as if he didn't quite believe his eyes.

Letting the gun muzzle droop even farther, Eben grinned. "I'm glad to see it's you."

"Huh?"

"I thought maybe it was trouble coming again," he offered in explanation. "Already had some trouble a few days ago. Ain't anxious for more."

Still shocked, Cully asked, "*You* ain't the one who's took up on this land?"

"I s'pose I am," Eben owned, his grin fading. "You're working for the man who means to run me off it?"

Cully nodded.

"You come here now to do it?"

"Couple of the fellers said they'd done it already. Said they'd scared the devil out of some barefoot dirt-grubber down here. Boss told me to ride over and see how much damage had been done to the land."

"No damage."

He looked sadly toward Eben's furrows. "You've cut it."

"Mean to plant it."

"Oh, hell!" The cowboy spread his open hands in an

almost pleading gesture. "Hawk, you *can't* farm down here. Mister Starrett won't have no part of it."

"He ain't got a say in it. This land don't belong to him. It belongs to the widow Hawkins."

"Kin of yours?"

"Was my brother's wife."

"Same brother you were looking for? He's dead?"

Eben nodded. He asked, "You mean to try running me off here for this Starrett?"

Studying on it, Cully grimaced at his own thoughts. He seemed to be having a hard time with them. Finally he gave a slow shake of his head. "No, not right now, I don't reckon. I got no orders to run you. Boss figured you'd be gone. Just told me to come and take a look at what you'd done here. The way them two bragged it up, he figured you'd lit out like a jackrabbit with its tail on fire."

Eben gestured with the rifle. "There ain't no point in Our fighting each other if we don't have to, is there?"

Cully shook his head. "I don't want to fight you."

"Why'n't you get up off your knees?"

He rose with his hands still spread out open. Realizing it, he looked embarrassed and let them drop to his sides. He didn't seem to know what to say or do next.

That gave Eben an odd feeling. He'd have expected himself to be the one who'd run out of words. But they were coming easy to him. And even if Cully was working for the rancher, he felt honestly glad to see the cowboy again.

He motioned toward the cabin. "If your boss wants you to see what I've done here, come on over and look. I got some work I want to get on with."

Cully followed behind him. Certain he was in no

84

danger for now, Eben leaned the gun against the wall and went over to grab hold of another log. He dragged it toward the front of the cabin.

Cully'd poked his head through the doorway. Turning toward Eben, he asked, "You done all this by yourself?"

"Floor was in," he grunted, hefting at the timber to get an end onto his shoulder. He got it and paused to draw a breath before he tried raising it from there into place. "I just been putting the walls up on it."

The cowboy still seemed impressed. "You been busy. You done all this and plowed that piece of field, too?"

"Yeah, only them friends of yours took off the ox 'fore I could finish it. Took my horse, too." Eben started to lift the log.

"You're wasting your time on this place. Mister Starrett ain't gonna let you stay," Cully eyed him. "What you trying to do there?"

"Get this thing on top the wall," he muttered, struggling with it.

"Hell," Cully grunted. Looking disgusted, he grabbed on and helped lift. The timber slid into place. Eben gave it a shove to seat the notches. Leaning against the wall, he wiped his forehead and grinned at Cully.

"You're wasting your time," the cowboy repeated. He rubbed his hands together as if to scrub the feel of the log off them. "You say they've left you here without a horse?"

"Yeah."

"What the hell you figure you can do without a horse?"

"Build a house." There was pride in Eben's grin as he hooked a thumb toward the wall. " 'Sides, I figure if they turned that old ox loose anywhere around here, it ought to come drifting back pretty soon now. I'll get on with my plowing then."

"That ain't a dark reddish sort of steer with a white tassel to its tail and real short horns? Roundish-built and getting on in years?"

He nodded.

"And your horse, is it a hammerheaded little lineback dun geld with a lot of white around the eye?"

"Yeah."

"Ain't neither one of them gonna come drifting back, Hawk," Cully said, shaking his head in discouragement. "The boys fetched them in up to the winter quarters. Got 'em penned up there. Likely gonna stay penned till the boss has word you've gone out the valley."

Eben looked toward the furrowed earth and the part of the field he hadn't touched yet. "Dammit, I *need* that ox!"

"It ain't *your* ox. You got no right to use it."

"That ain't Starrett's horse either. Them men of his hadn't any right to take it away from me."

"Why'd you let 'em do it?" Cully glanced toward the rifle as if it should have settled the question.

"I wasn't expecting the way they come at me. That Pete one can do some pretty fancy things with a piece of rope." Ropes seemed to be part of a cowboy's stock in trade. Eben had noticed that there was one coiled on Cully's saddle, too. Curious, he asked, "Can you do stuff like that?"

"Like what? Anything that Pete can do with a throw rope, I can do twice better."

"Can you throw it from off the back of your horse and loop a man on the run? Haul him down and make your horse hold him?"

"Sure. I never done it, though." Cully looked at him, frowning slightly. "Pete do that to you?"

"Yeah."

"Drag you any?"

"Not much," he muttered, shaking his head. He felt an anger at himself for having let that happen. There sure hadn't been any warning what to expect, though. The cowboys had outwitted and outnumbered him every which way that time. He didn't mean to let it happen again, though.

He asked, "Is that how they killed my brother?"

"Huh? What the hell you mean by that?"

"It was cowboys who killed Jake, wasn't it? It was by order of this Starrett, wasn't it?"

"No! I never heard nothing like that. What give you such a notion?"

"They say Jake was dragged to death. Could have been by a rope just as easy as by a stirrup. 'Specially if someone was looking to kill him."

Cully scowled darkly. "When'd this happen?"

"'Round Christmas. His wife found his body. She says they'd been threatened to get off this land."

"That's raw," he muttered, studying on it. With a firm shake of his head, he said, "I don't hold none with murder. Not no how! I know some that do, though."

Struck with a sudden new thought, he looked sideways at Eben. "It true you stuck a knife in that Jasper feller over to Cheyenne?"

Was that an accusation of murder, Eben wondered. He said slowly, "Yeah, but I didn't kill him. The lawman told me he wasn't hurt bad."

"He wasn't. He's working for Mister Starrett now. If he finds out you're setting down here in this hole all by your lonesome, he'll be right happy to come quarter you and spit your liver over a slow fire."

"You mean Starrett'll send him down to kill me?"

*"No!"* Cully protested. "Mister Starrett ain't the killing type. I don't care what you say about this brother of yours, Mister Starrett ain't the kind to up and murder a man like that!"

"Sure, he's a real kindly sort who only just burns houses and tramples fields and . . ."

"I'll allow he's quick to boil and firm in his notions and maybe sometimes a little rough in the way he gets things done. But I sure can't see him doing no killing. Leastways, not slow and mean, like dragging a man to death."

"What about his hired hands?"

"The fellers do what the boss tells 'em," he answered, as if it were a law of nature.

"You, too?"

"Me, too. Only not murder!"

Eben stood silent, gazing into the distance, thinking of sudden death. A man could feel justified in killing and not feel like it was murder at all.

"The boss is gonna tell us to run you off of here, Hawk," Cully said.

"I ain't leaving."

"There ain't nothing much you can do here without a horse, even if the boss was to let you be."

"I've been giving that some thought," Eben muttered. He looked toward the cabin, determined to get it finished. The front wall only needed one more log, and it was ready. Starting to fetch it, he said, "You want to help me get another timber up?"

Cully worked his mouth and spat. He grumbled something deep in his throat but he gave a hand.

As they hefted the log into place, Eben asked him, "What's this winter quarters place you say my horse and ox are at?"

"Just that," he grunted. "Winter quarters."

"But what is it?"

"Don't you know nothing about the cow business around here?"

"No."

They settled the log. He scrubbed his hands together, then wiped them down his thighs. Taking a deep breath, as if he had a long tale to string out, he began. "Well, now, summertime Mister Starrett runs his beeves in the high grass over yonder ways. He's got the main house over that way, near to Cheyenne, and he lives there then and bosses over things himself all summer. Come fall, though, we move the beeves in this direction. This valley's the best piece of winter range around here. So he's got a place near to here for headquarters in the winter."

"He lives there then?" Eben asked.

Cully grinned as if it were a fool question. "Mister Starrett? He winters in some city like St. Louis or New Orleans or something. Leaves the *primero* live at the winter quarters to run things. Stays there himself awhile during spring cow-hunting, though. He's up there right now. And when I tell him you're still squatting here on his range, he ain't gonna be happy about it."

"I don't care is he happy. Where is this winter quarters of his?"

"What you want to know for?" He eyed Eben with sudden suspicion. "You ain't planning on going up there to augur him, are you? I can tell you now . . ."

"No. I ain't much good with talk."

"Then what do you figure to do?"

Eben gave him no answer.

He mulled, then asked, "You ain't got some notion of taking back your horse?"

"I got a notion he ain't entitled to keep it penned against my will. And if that ox was to get loose, too, maybe that wouldn't be none of my concern."

Cully looked incredulous. "You're crazy!"

There'd been a time when that word had an edge that cut like a knife. No matter how it might be said, even in fun. it would have cut deep enough to hurt bad. But Eben realized with surprise that this time it didn't bother him at all. He knew exactly what he wanted to do, and felt a certainty that he could do it. Even if the idea was crazy, that didn't seem to matter.

He grinned at the cowboy and said, "Crazy as a hoot owl."

"Hawk," Cully said solemnly, "I can't hold that Mister Starrett would do a murder just to get you off this land. But you go messing around, he'll fight you. And a man can get killed awful easy in that kind of fighting."

"Might be you should tell that to Starrett."

"Hell, I don't want to see you get trampled and scattered for the buzzards. You sure seem to have your mind set on it, though."

"Yeah."

"Ain't there no turning you?"

"You ever try to turn a cannonball once the lanyard's pulled?"

He shook his head. Reluctantly, he told Eben, "Ranch house is about three, four hours ride from here. Further'n that if you're afoot, I reckon. You just go up that way," he pointed off past the bluff, "till you come to wagon tracks. You follow 'em straight along. They run right to the house."

Eben realized he meant the trail Alice had called the ranch road. Hell, he thought, he should have figured that out for himself. He asked, "You gonna tell Starrett what

I got in mind?"

"He ain't asked me yet. if he don't, I reckon I won't have no call to mention it. But you got to understand, he's my boss. It's him who gave me work when I first come up to this part of the country. It's him as has hired me on three years now, and I'll do what he tells me. If he says to me I got to come back and run you off, I'll do it. You understand that?"

It was plain enough. When an officer gave a man an order, he obeyed it. Even if it was to send a blast of canister tearing through the same bunch of Rebs he'd swapped coffee and news with the night before, he still did it. He might be sorry of it, but he did it.

Eben nodded. "Sure, I understand. Only you know I'll fight back?"

"You would," Cully said with conviction. "You wouldn't do nothing else. Get yourself hurt, maybe killed, just for a damned piece of land."

"Ain't just the land."

"What the hell is it, then?"

"It ain't nothing I could explain in words," Eben muttered, looking off across the fields at the peaks that gashed jaggedly into the sky.

"He's just as damnfool stubborn. With him it's his beeves and his grass. You spit on one of his beeves or bruise a blade of his grass, he'll carry on like it was him himself you'd done it to. He's thunder and lightning, Hawk, and you can't no more hold him off than you could a raging storm."

There were thunderheads built up far beyond the peaks. They sparkled in the sunlight, bright and pure-looking as fresh-fallen snow. But he knew what one could do when it turned gray and opened up on a man. Softly, he repeated, "I'll fight him."

91

"Damned waste," Cully sighed. With a shake of his head, he eyed the cabin. "G'damned helluva waste."

Turning slowly, as if he were aching with weariness, he stalked toward his horse. Eben watched him mount up and pull the horse around. With a quick glance back, he gigged the animal into a hard gallop upvalley.

Man fought a war because he had to, Eben thought as he headed back to the cabin. Not because it was something he wanted to do, but because he *had* to. Come a time he had to do a killing, he did it. No matter what it might cost him.

The next morning he pulled on his boots and checked over the rifle and the pocket pistol. Carrying them both, he set out for the ranch road.

# CHAPTER 8

IT WAS LATE IN THE AFTERNOON WHEN EBEN FINALLY caught sight of the ranch. He worked his way cautiously through the edges of the woods, studying on it. Then he picked a spot and settled down to wait for darkness.

The buildings were set in a clearing along the foot of a gentle slope. One was a long, skinny log structure that looked like a pair of cabins built a bit apart, with the space between them walled and roofed. All three sections had doors. The end ones had small windows, too. A stovepipe stuck up from each end, one showing faint threads of smoke.

He figured it for living quarters of some kind. The windows had glass panes. There were water barrels and a bench with a wash basin, a mirror, and a towel, near the door.

Paths were worn through the grass from the doors. One led straight down to the outhouse. Another crossed the slope toward a cluster of pole-fenced pens. The two big pens had horses and a few mules in them. The red ox stood alone in one of the smaller pens. He couldn't see his horse among the bunches, but he wasn't much concerned about that. It was the ox he wanted.

There were other outbuildings and sheds, and upslope a ways, a stone house. It was about twice the size of the cabin he'd been building. The windows flanking the front door had heavy-looking shutters latched open. The wide-caved roof tripped up to a thick stone chimney. There was no smoke.

He figured the stone house was where Starrett lived when he was staying here at winter quarters. It didn't look like anyone was around right now, though. Didn't look like anyone was anywhere on the place. He wondered if he could go ahead and do what he had in mind now, instead of waiting for night. The traces of smoke from that one stovepipe kept him cautious, though. It might only be a fire left banked to save the coals, but he wanted to be damn sure before he went drifting down there.

He lay on his belly in the brush, with the rifle in the crook of his arm. Motionless, just watching and waiting, he began to recollect times he'd lain in wait for game when he was a boy.

He remembered the old squirrel gun with affection. It had been a long-barreled, heavy-muzzled Pennsylvania rifle, and for years it had stood taller than he did. An awkward thing, especially to load, but he'd got the hang of handling it. He'd managed to put more than a little meat in the pot with it.

There were a lot of good memories. The smell of the

mountains in the spring. The cool pleasure of splashing in the pool under the waterfall on a hot summer's day. The turning colors of fall. The way the winter snow would glitter and sparkle under a bright sun. The feel of coming into a kitchen warm with the scents of baking after he'd been out trekking through that snow. Hot corn cakes with honey.

He recalled the time a bear had tried to raid the bee gums and he'd taken a shot at it. It had gotten so excited that it blundered straight into the kitchen. It made a line right through the house and out the front door, leaving a trail of busted-up furniture and things behind it. Afterward, he'd been told off for not minding out which way he chased it, but his pa'd been laughing all the while. Remembering, he grinned to himself.

The afternoon was drifting lazily into evening. He watched the ranch, wondering if anyone was down there. The ox in the pen seemed to be waiting too. It stood with its head pressed against a rail, unmoving except for the steady swinging of the white tassel at the end of its tail. He wondered if animals had thoughts.

"You just think on repenting your sin, old cow," he said silently. "You got a midnight pardon coming when it's dark enough."

Something at the log building caught his eye. He wasn't sure whether or not he'd actually seen a flicker of motion behind one of those glass windows. Tense, he waited.

The door opened and a man came out carrying a bushel. He set it down, settled himself on the bench, yawned, and stretched. Then he took a potato from the bushel and began to peel it.

Eben eased back, getting comfortable. It looked like he wasn't mistaken in waiting for darkness after all.

94

After a time the man at the bench finished his work and took his potatoes back inside. The smoke from the stovepipe thickened. Evidently that end of the log building was a cookhouse.

Twilight came on. The bugs that swarmed around him got worse. He batted at them, envying the ox its handy built-in fly swatter and wishing time would pass so he could get on with his chore.

The wind brought him scents of cooking. Sniffing at them, he realized he hadn't eaten for a fair long time. Not since breakfast. He was hungry. But there were more important things to concern himself with.

The shadows grew longer and mistier, blending together as the sun disappeared behind the ridges. It got hard to see clearly. He heard the horses coming before he spotted them.

The way the riders were clumped up, he couldn't tell just how many there were. About half a dozen he guessed. He wondered if that was all of Starrett's crew. They tended their mounts, then went into the cookhouse. Lit lamps inside silhouetted each of them as he walked through the doorway. Eben counted seven of them then. He didn't think any of them was Cully. But this was the place, all right.

He waited, but no more men showed up. That got him to wondering if Starrett had another camp of some kind. He wished he knew more about this ranching business. He had no idea how large a force Starrett could muster.

It was full dark, with a scattering of stars giving faint light, when the cookhouse door opened. Two men headed up toward the stone house together. Several more came out into the yard. They stood around smoking and talking. He couldn't make out their words.

Eventually they took their walks down the hill, then

came back and went into the other end of the building. Light showed through its windows awhile. They were snuffed out before the ones up at the stone house. But finally the last light disappeared. The ranch was peacefully, quietly dark.

Eben studied the stars as he waited. He let what he figured to be a couple of hours go by before he moved.

With the cocked rifle in his hand, he headed silently down the slope.

There was a feeling of ice lying along his spine. It chilled him to slow, shallow breathing and cautious footsteps. He could hear vividly, as if every small sound in the night was as sharp-drawn as a bow across a fiddle string. Pesks sang in the grass. Small things scurried through it. Somewheres off a ways an owl called out, low and lonesome as the railroad whistles he'd been able to hear from his cell. He shivered slightly.

From the log building, he could hear sounds of snoring, like a bank of steam saws, and the creaking of bed frames. Reassuring sounds. He moved past them toward the pens.

A horse gave a small tentative nicker. Hoofs shuffled as the animals stirred uneasily. They knew he was there. He hoped they didn't object to strangers prowling around them in the night.

Staying as far away from the horses as he could, he made his way to the gate of the pen with the ox in it. He slung the rifle over his shoulder and used both hands to ease it open. Even so, the squeak of it sounded godawful loud in the night.

The ox didn't seem to notice him until he scrubbed his fingers under its chin. Then it stretched out its head to welcome his attention. He'd brought a pocketful of corn to lure it. Just a taste and it ambled along after him without the need of more coaxing. It seemed pleased to follow him to freedom. But he couldn't urge it into anything faster than a slow plodding.

The walk leading it across the slope seemed a lot longer than the walk down had been. It was stringing out his nerves way worse. He felt almost overwhelmed with relief when he finally reached the woods.

The ox pressed its forehead against his arm, begging for more petting. As he let it lick corn off his hand, he wondered if he really wanted to go back and finish what he'd planned. He had the ox. Maybe he should be satisfied with that. Maybe he shouldn't take the chance of losing it again tonight.

But he was certain those cowboys would be back to see him. Last time they'd just dragged him down to the dirt and made threatening talk. Next time they'd try to do worse. Likely they'd devil him just as hard whether he stood still for it or fought back. And he'd come here tonight meaning to show them that he intended to fight back.

He led the ox a good ways along the road, then dumped the rest of the corn out of his pocket onto the ground. He left the ox busy tonguing it up and headed back toward the ranch.

The slope seemed to have stretched while he wasn't looking. This trip across it felt twice as far as the last one. He swung wide of the log house and came up toward the horse pens with the wind in his face.

The horses stirred restlessly as he approached them. They shuffled back to the far side of the pen. He could sense them eying him with distrust.

Upslope, near the stone house, a dog gave out a volley of short, uncertain yaps. He froze, waiting for a reaction.

Nothing happened. At last he eased out the held breath, took another, and slung the rifle over his shoulder. Cautiously, he worked the gate open a ways. Not far, though. He didn't want the horses discovering it too soon. He had to get over to that other pen.

The dog called out again, questioning the night. But it sounded like it was still in the same place. Maybe it was just noising about some critter that had ventured too close up there.

He touched his hand to the gate of the second pen. And just then a horse found the one he'd already opened. It bolted through. The rest of the bunch lit out after it, hoofs drumming like a charge of cavalry.

The horses in this pen began to mill, snuffling and snorting. Some of them spooked. They flung themselves against the poles.

Heedless of noise now, Eben slammed open the gate. A horse lunged toward it.

From the log house, someone hollered, "What the hell's happening!"

Horses thundered past him as he pressed up against the gatepost. Beyond them, he glimpsed light. A door of the log house was open. Men dashed through it.

He leaped for the nearest horse. Grabbing for its flowing mane, he jumped at its back. It was smaller than the artillery horses had been. The catch was easy. So was hauling himself up onto it. But getting a seat wasn't.

With a frantic snort, the pony jerked down its head and heaved its rump. Clinging to the mane, he felt himself pitched forward.

He was in the middle of the bunch Their pounding hoofs surrounded him. He didn't want to come off the pony. He didn't dare—

Its shoulders rose, twisting, as its back arched. He was sliding sideways. For an instant, he was sure he had come loose.

His fingers were locked into the pony's mane. He felt himself flung with a force that snapped at his arm joints. But he hung on.

The pony might have pitched harder if it hadn't been trying to keep up with the rest of the bunch at the same time. For a couple of strides, it concentrated on running. In that moment, he got himself righted, his legs firm to its sides. Settled, he bent low over its withers. It heaved its spine again, but this time he was set on its back; and prepared for trouble. He stayed put.

The horses were running wild, stringing out across the slope. They hit the woods like cannon fire, crashing through the underbrush. He heard a sharp snap that might have been a dry branch under a hoof. Or maybe a gunshot at a distance. In the thunder the horses roused, he couldn't be sure.

Pushing through the woods, the pony began to slow. The panic that had set it flying in frenzy was easing. Eben watched for his chance. As soon as it seemed safe, he slid off.

Letting his knees flex as he hit ground, he managed to keep to his feet. He staggered to a tree and leaned against it, drawing deep breaths. He was weary— outright exhausted—but he felt just fine. Scrubbing one hand across his sweating face, he grinned with satisfaction. Those cowboys would be busy for a while hunting their horses. After that, they'd likely be hunting *him*. They'd find him, too—with a gun ready in his hands.

He started back through the woods, keeping to cover alongside the ranch road. The sun was coming up when

99

he reached the cabin again.

Before he'd left to go up to Starrett's, he'd stashed away his grub and gear in the crannies of the scarp. He dug out a couple of airtights and took them to the ledge overlooking the farm. Settling there, he knifed them open and washed down the cold, mushy beans with juice from the peaches. With his belly satisfied, he stretched out holding the rifle in his arms and let himself sleep.

Something woke him suddenly. He wasn't sure what it had been. Lying still, he listened, but he didn't hear anything unusual. Cautiously, he squirmed forward until he could look down from the ledge.

The ox was nosing around the cabin.

Grinning to himself, he slumped back and rested his head on his arm. In a moment, he was asleep again.

The sun hung low over the ridges by the time he woke, feeling rested. Below, the ox had drifted off to browse the grass of the bottoms. In the distance, cattle moved along the fringes of the woods. Scanning them, he spotted an elk on the high slopes. But there was no sign of men.

Feeling damned satisfied with himself and ready for whatever might come, he fetched more food and got comfortable on the ledge again while he ate. He knew he should be unhappy about the waste of good working time that this business with Starrett was costing him. But it was a lot of years since he'd been free to stand up and fight back when someone flung an order at him that he didn't fancy. He took a deep pleasure in the feel of having done it. He was nigh looking forward to doing it again.

He enjoyed sitting there on his perch watching night creep into the valley. It began with misty blue shadows that stretched slowly until they filled the whole of the basin. Across the way, sunlight still caught at the peaks, giving a golden tint to the high snow. As it faded, the sky behind them darkened. A star poked its light through the deep glowing purple. It grew stronger and others joined it. The mountains became jagged black gashes in the edge of the soft-lit sky.

The sounds changed from the busy chatter of the day into the more cautious whispers of darkness. Night animals made specks of sound that were like stars. Crisp and clear as they were, they didn't interrupt the steady silence around them any more than stars marred the night sky.

Yawning, he stretched. His shirt pulled snug at the shoulders. He'd been putting on weight here in the valley. He wondered if he could fill out that coat of Jake's now.

As the thought went through his mind, it struck a spark of anger. Dammit, he didn't want to fill Jake's coat or take Jake's place. He wasn't Jake. He was *Eben.* Let 'em remember that. They shouldn't look to him to be like Jake. Even if he could, he wouldn't. Right or wrong, good or bad, he was *Eben* and that was who he wanted to be.

Something howled in the distance. He thought it was one of those doggish animals called a coyote. It had a strange almost-human voice. The cry gave him a shivery, apprehensive feeling.

Frowning intently, he listened. The silence that followed the call seemed deep and unnatural. He realized that some of the night animals had stopped muttering to themselves. It was as if some of the stars had blinked out, leaving blank gaps in the sky.

Stars disappeared when something stood between you

and them. Night animals hushed when something came too close.

Picking up the rifle, Eben shifted onto one knee. The way the scarp cupped around the ledge, he knew no one could skylight him. Even by day a person would have a hard time spotting anyone on the ledge from below.

Fine-drawn and ready, he waited.

There were soft brushing noises. Something creaked like saddle leather. A small metallic clink was as sharp as lightning.

Placing the sounds, he guessed the men to be spread out in a wide arc along the edges of the forest. Sneaking up on him, he thought, grinning.

He glimpsed a shadow moving in the darkness. A twig cracked. Close by, a horse snuffled. Each faint sound was distinct in the stillness. Breathing softly, he waited.

A sudden yelping shout jerked the lanyard.

Riders exploded from the woods, hollering like the Reb cavalry in full charge. They thundered across the fields to converge on the cabin.

Screaming and shooting, they strung out in a circle around it. Their waving handguns filled the night with orange flares and the stink of burnt powder.

From the look of it, they were shooting into the air, not at the cabin. They seemed to be trying to scare the devil out of anyone inside, but not trying to kill. At least not yet.

They were galloping wildly around the cabin, raising all hell. He knelt on the ledge, watching them and enjoying the spectacle. Sniffing at the burnt powder, he thought of the waste of it and good lead and all the energy the cowboys were putting into their attack. If they kept it up like this for long, he figured they weren't going to have much pepper left for whatever work they had to do in the morning. The horses sure weren't.

He wondered if it had occurred to them that a man inside that cabin just might try shooting back. Admittedly, they'd be hard targets the way they were riding, but one could get himself hit by accident. They had nerve, he allowed. And they were sure damned fine riders. They underestimated their enemy, though. From the way they acted, none of 'em had figured he might have expected this raid and planned for it.

After a few more gallops around, one of the men jerked his horse into a rear. Waving, he swung it and headed off away from the cabin. The others followed.

They regrouped at a distance, all bunching together. He could hear them murmuring, sounding disappointed.

As he watched, he amused himself by judging range and elevation. A load of canister from his ledge could have cut down the lot of them. He wished he had a fieldpiece here. It'd have been fun to drop a solid shot in front of them. Let it bounce and roll toward them. He could imagine them scattering like hens from a hawk.

They finished their confab and began to work slowly back toward the cabin. After they'd nosed around a bit, satisfying themselves that it was empty, they bunched again. This time they were close under Eben's perch.

In a strong voice, with the tone of a man used to commanding, one of them called out, "All right, boys, light up the torches."

*Oh, no, you don't,* Eben thought, settling the rifle butt against his shoulder. He looked along the barrel, trying to pick out which one of the dark figures had given the order.

Matches sputtered. He waited, watching the flames leap up and spread across the torch heads. The light played wildly over them, showing them to him clearly. He figured it would probably confuse their eyes bad.

"All right," their commander hollered. Eben spotted him then. A small, wiry man with shoulders too wide for the rest of him. The horse he was on danced nervously, and the firelight shimmered over its sweated hide. It looked half-wild, maybe a little crazy. He held a tight rein, but gave it no more attention than that. Waving toward the cabin, he started, "Go ahead and—"

"Hold it, mister!" Eben shouted. "There's a Henry rifle sighted square on you!"

He could feel their shock in the moment of silence. Heads jerked, and faces turned up to stare toward the scarp. He couldn't pick out Cully among them. Or Jasper either. He was glad for that.

"What!" the wiry man grunted, squinting futilely at the shadowed rocks. "Who—?"

"I'm Eben Hawkins. One of you Mister Starrett?"

"I am," he answered. "Are you the damn fool who's been cutting up my land?"

"It ain't your land," Eben said. "Least not the piece you're standing on. S'pose you take your men and get off it. Go back where you come from and leave me be."

"This valley's *mine!*"

"Unh-unh. This here quarter section belongs to Jake Hawkins' widow. I'm holding it for her."

"This is *my* land—"

"By what right?"

Starrett ignored him. "—and I won't have no damned dirt-grubber tearing it up, ruining my grass!"

"By what right you think it's yours?" Eben repeated.

"Possession! I got it and I mean to keep it."

"No, sir!" he shook his head, though he knew they couldn't see him. "*I* got this land and I'm holding it. No, sir, Mosby, you ain't taking it. I'll give you six foot of hell first."

Starrett hesitated, puzzled. He called, "My name ain't Mosby."

"Maybe not," Eben allowed. He'd crossed up the times again. Not in his thinking though—only on his tongue. And he knew why it had happened. "Knew a feller once we called Mosby. Back in Andersonville. We named him that after the Reb raider."

"Huh?" Starrett gazed up at the rocks, frowning.

The memories were stirring strong in Eben. He went on, "You see how it was; this feller, Mosby, had a bunch of friends. They were prisoners, too, but they went around attacking the other prisoners. Stealing food and stuff off 'em. A man'd be too sick or weak to defend himself, they'd rob him naked. They'd beat a man to death for a handful of cornmeal. You put me in mind of him, Starrett."

"Goddammit, Hawkins, I—!"

"We got him, though. We started up our own police and caught him and some of his bunch. We judged 'em and hanged 'em there in the stockade." The images were vivid in his mind, the words sharp-edged in his mouth. He spat them at Starrett.

"We hanged some of 'em then and there. Others— one I got later. Sliced his lights out with a knife. Spilled 'em out of him while he watched. More'n once I'd had the food took out of my hand when I was too fevered to help myself. Only I ain't sick now, Starrett. And you ain't taking this land from me."

There was silence. In it, he heard the shuffling of the restless horses, the soft jangle of bit chains, the shifting groan of leather.

The torches sputtered as if they whispered among

themselves. Their light leaped across Starrett's staring face, mocking twisted grimaces on it.

Eben felt fires within himself. He'd roused them with his talking, his remembering. Now he felt almost feverish with them. Lightheaded and wild. *Crazy,* he told himself. But he didn't care. He wanted to fight, to beat this man who threatened to steal his dreams.

He broke the silence. The rifle was already cocked, but he levered up another cartridge, watching their faces as they heard and recognized the sharp clicking of the action.

Starrett winced. The man nearest him started a hand for the pistol he wore. One of the others jerked rein so hard that his horse reared.

"I never killed a man with a rifle," Eben said quietly. "Maybe you ought to get off *my* land 'fore I take a notion to try it."

The rancher's hands were taut on the reins. He held the excited horse hard up on the bit. Its mouth gaped open and its jaw was up against its chest.

His face twisted. He seemed to be struggling something inside himself. When he finally spoke, he had his voice tight-reined, too. He made it soft and cadging.

"Look, boy, I don't want to hurt you or steal anything from you. This *ain't* your land, but if you got some notion it is, then I'll buy it off you. I'll settle you a fair price for it. You just come on down and talk to me peaceably."

Eben frowned in surprise. The man sounded sincere. He seemed like he was really willing to bargain for the land.

But Eben wasn't. He answered, "No, sir! Mister Starrett, all I want is this here quarter section. That's all

I'm taking. You got the whole rest of this valley and a hell of a lot more land outside it where you can keep your beeves. You ain't gonna miss a hundred sixty acres."

"Ain't just a quarter section." The rancher shook his head firmly. "First it's you. Then it's somebody else. Next thing I know, the whole valley'll be plowed up and planted over. All my grass ruined. I can't have that."

"You can't stop it. Government says this land's free to us who'll work it. Land-office paper says this here piece of ground belongs to Miz Hawkins. I mean to work it for her," Eben said.

*"It's mine!"* Starrett was struggling to hold on to his temper. The words were snagging in his throat. "I've got it, and I've already fought you damned dirt-grubbers to keep it, I've run out plow-pushers before you, boy. You make me do it, and I'll run you out the same way!"

"You mean to murder me the way you did my brother Jake?"

"That was—dammit! I don't know nothing about your brother Jake!"

"That was *what?"*

"That was—something I don't know nothing about," he answered weakly. "I don't know what you're talking about."

"Jacob Hawkins. The feller who built the last cabin you tried to burn off this land. The feller you dragged to death behind a horse."

"Damn you, Hawkins! This is your last chance! You come down here and talk decent with me, I'll pay you off. Else I'll *run* you off."

"Try it!" Eben dropped his sights. He squeezed the trigger, sending lead slamming into the earth just in front of Starrett's horse. Dirt spattered. The horse gave a

107

panicked snort. Fighting the bit, it reared. Its hoofs shot out, pawing wildly. The reins were too short. The frenzied animal overbalanced. Clawing air, it toppled backward.

Starrett flung himself out of the saddle. Arms flailing, he spilled on the ground. The breath slammed out of him in a sharp gust.

Scrambling up, the horse bolted. A rider wheeled to chase after it. As he raced out of the firelight, Eben saw him swinging his rope into a loop.

Starrett gasped breath as he propped himself up.

"You *like* grubbing dirt?" Eben called at him.

One of the cowboys had jumped down to help him. He snapped angrily at the man and hauled himself to his feet. As the rider came up leading his horse, he grabbed at it.

Hefting himself jerkily to its back, he looked toward the scarp again. He was almost shaking with anger. His eyes hunted among the shadows. Eben could feel the probing touch of them, like fire. But they passed by him. The darkness covered him.

Starrett twisted in the saddle and pointed toward the cabin. "*Burn it!*"

Eben spanged lead against the log wall.

The men with the torches hesitated.

Scowling fiercely at the mountain, Starrett screamed, "I'll get you! Damn you, Hawkins, I'll get you!"

Eben let the rifle answer for him. The slug whined as it ricocheted off the wall.

With a jab of spurs that brought a pained snort from the horse, Starrett lunged it into a run. He waved, calling, and the others galloped after him. The ones with torches flung them down. They fell, still burning, on the bare earth.

Resting the rifle across his knees, Eben watched them flicker and burn out.

# CHAPTER 9

Dawn came, bringing fresh, clean breezes and rousing the cheery sounds of the daylight animals. The sun poked brightly over the eastern ridges. It spilled the warm gold of its light into the valley. The old ox waited patiently beside the cabin, hoping for a handful of corn and some petting.

It all looked different now. The torches lay dead on the hoof-turned earth. A fresh edge of the lead embedded in the cabin wall was like a spark in the sunlight.

Eben walked slowly over the land with the rifle slung on his shoulder and his hands thrust deep into his pockets. He pondered the night that seemed more like something he'd dreamed than lived. It was a fever dream. But its relics were real. He pried the bit of lead out of the log with his knife. Holding it in his hand, he studied on it, then pocketed it.

He felt depressed, vaguely shamed, by what had happened. He couldn't see much other way things could have gone, though. Not without he surrendered to Starrett. And he had no notion of doing that.

The ox ambled up to him and prodded gently at his arm. He scratched it around the ears, feeling a kind of comfort in its company. It didn't judge him or ask anything of him but a share of his food and a bit of petting. Its mild eyes looked on him solemnly, as if its head were full of wisdom. But there was no reproach in them.

"You reckon I shoulda bargained that feller last night?" he said aloud. The ox gazed at him. "You think maybe Miz Alice would sooner I'd took his money and left off this land?"

The ox twisted its neck and licked at his arm. He slid his fingers under its chin, roughing them into the stubby hair.

"I got a way of forgetting it ain't *my* land. It's *hers.* Maybe I ain't got the right to decide as much as I been doing. Maybe I ain't got the wit for it."

There was no answer to be had from the animal. Eben wiped his hand against his pants leg. He looked up at the slopes that were still peaked with snow and out across the bottoms springing green with wild grasses. Sighing, he said, "I wish to hell it was mine."

The ox nudged at him, eager for more petting. But he'd sparked a thought for himself that took all his attention. He leaned an arm on the ox's back as he studied on it.

Suddenly he grinned. Giving the ox a shove, he said "Old cow, you're gonna have to take care of yourself for a while. I think I got business in Cheyenne."

It gazed at him as he hurried to pack himself a few supplies for the walk to Garrison. With the bundle on his shoulder and the rifle in his hand, he set out toward the town.

He was too alive with his own thoughts to sleep that night. After he'd rested awhile, he got back to walking. By sunup he was trudging down the slope to the street.

He stopped at the town pump and heaved the handle a few times. Cupping his hands under the spout, he caught the last gushes of water and slapped them into his face. There was a week's worth of beard on his jaw, but he'd been too concerned with other things to worry over it.

He still was. He hoped that water would take some of the dirt off his face, but mostly he wanted the cold shock of it to sharpen his thinking. He had to see Alice and ask a favor of her. That was the only part of the whole idea that bothered him.

He headed for the back door of the lodging house and settled himself on the kitchen steps, waiting to hear some sounds of people moving around inside before he knocked.

Resting, he half-dozed in spite of the excitement in him. The sudden click of the latch jerked him awake just in time to duck the door swinging open. He jumped up, wheeling toward it.

Alice had a bucket in her hand. She'd already started to fling out the water, just as she saw him. In an instant, he glimpsed the bucket in motion and her startled face. He blinked. And he was sopping wet.

"Oh, my! Oh, Eben!"

He couldn't tell from the sound of it whether she was crying or laughing. Wiping at his eyes with his sleeve, he looked at her, but he couldn't be sure from her face either. She had her hand pressed up to her mouth, and her eyes were wide. She seemed like maybe she didn't know which to do.

He grinned at her.

She laughed then. "Oh, Eben, I'm sorry! I didn't know you were there."

"I hope not. I'd sooner think you didn't do that apurpose."

"Come in." Smiling, she held the door open to him. "Take off that wet coat. There's a fire in the stove."

The kitchen smelled of biscuits baking and ham frying. The scents stirred his juices. He looked at the big slabs of meat sizzling in pans on the range. It was the largest cookstove he'd ever seen. Peeling the wet coat, he stepped up into its warmth. The water'd hit him in the face, and some had run down his collar, but his coat had caught most of it. Alice grabbed it out of his hands. She hauled a chair toward the stove and draped it over the back to dry.

"That'll be ready by the time breakfast is served," she said. "If it isn't, nobody'll object to your eating in your shirt sleeves. Not in this town."

He thought of his problem again. "Ma'am, I got no money left."

"Oh? The things you bought when you were in before—? Eben, why did you go off without seeing me again?"

"Did you want me to see you?"

"Of course." She turned away to busy herself with her cooking, but she kept on talking. "Did you spend all your own money on those tools and things? Mister Beasley told me what you'd bought from him. He said he offered you terms in my name, but you insisted on paying him."

"Yes'm, only—" He hesitated. Stepping back, he tried to find a place to stand where he wouldn't be in her way. She scurried around the kitchen, her hands dancing through the things they did. He admired them as he watched.

"Ma'am," he began again. "I think I'm gonna have to ask you for the lend of some money."

"I'll pay you back what you've spent on the farm."

"No, ma'am, I only want the lend of some. Not much."

"But, Eben, that's silly. It's *my* farm. I can't afford to pay you hire, but I'll certainly pay for the things you need to work it. I make a good wage here. And I have the money Jake left me. You saw it."

He nodded, recalled the little poke of gold coins she had hidden in with Jake's belongings. There'd been a couple of eagles and a big fifty-dollar California cartwheel. A fair amount of money, but money she shouldn't be spending if she didn't have to. It was her security against troubles.

"First off, I got to tell you some things as have happened."

She looked at him questioningly.

He didn't want her to know about the bad parts of it. He skipped over a lot, just telling her he'd been visited by Starrett and that the rancher had offered to buy the land off him. When he asked her if she wanted to take Starrett's money and forget the farm, she looked solemnly into his eyes.

"What do *you* want to do?" she said.

"It ain't mine to decide. The land's yours."

"No, Eben, it's a *man's* decision. If Starrett has threatened you—you're the one who's living there, holding the land. Do you want to keep on?"

"I mean to stay in that valley, no matter what," he told her. "That quarter section's yours, but according to this Homestead thing, it might be I could claim a piece in my own name. I mean to go into Cheyenne and find out if that'd be lawful. If you want to let Starrett have your hold, that's up to you."

She gave him a small, wistful smile. "He isn't offering to buy *my* land, Eben. He's offering to pay you to leave the valley. It's a different thing."

He hadn't considered that. But he knew she was right. Nodding, he muttered, "Yeah, I s'pose that's so."

"If you want to stay in the valley, I think we should keep the land Jake claimed," she went on. "He said it was the best piece there. If you want it for yourself, I think we could—"

"No, ma'am. I don't want to take your land. I just want to work this out somehow. I want to stay in that valley. If I can get a hold of my own, I will. But if I can't, I'll work your land."

"Then that's settled." She smiled.

He wasn't so sure of that. There were things he'd said and done, acting in her name. He blurted out, "Ma'am, I threatened Starrett. Told him I might kill him."

"Did you mean it?" Her voice was thin, her face suddenly very serious.

"Yes'm," he owned. "If it comes a time I have to, I will. Was a time once before I had to kill a man. I done it." He felt no pride in the admission. But it was the truth of the matter.

Staring at his hands, he added, "Maybe you'd sooner be clear of it all, lest it happens."

"But no matter what I say or do, you mean to stay in the valley?"

He nodded.

"Jake used to say a man did what he had to," she said softly.

"So'd Pa."

"Jake died. He may have been murdered."

He nodded again. Still gazing at his hands, he muttered, "I might—it might come to such again."

She was silent a long, thoughtful moment. Then, quietly, wistfully, she said, "There are things I don't really understand about a *man's* ways of things. But I know that a man like Jake—like you—you'll do what you feel you have to, won't you, Eben? No matter what anyone says, you'll go by your own lights."

"Yes'm."

114

Her smile was small and tender. "It's *our* land, Eben. I wish I could help you with the working of it. And the fighting for it."

He looked into her eyes, reading her concern in the golden-brown depths of them. She'd a lot sooner he gave up the valley and kept away from the trouble that was stirring. But she gave him her trust and accepted his decision. He felt a puzzlement at that and a warm pleasure in it. She was an uncommon understanding woman, he thought. A damn fine woman.

It was late in the day when he dropped off the cars outside Cheyenne with a gold eagle and a handful of small coins in his pocket. He'd managed to ride without paying the brakeman's toll this time. Hoping he wasn't too late to find it open, he hurried in search of the land office.

The door was latched, but through the glass panes he could see a man studying over some papers. When he gave a rap, the man looked up and gestured for him to go away. He knocked again and rattled impatiently at the latch.

Finally the man opened the door a crack and grunted, "Go 'way! I'm closed for the day."

"You're still here, though," Eben said, leaning against the door to keep him from closing it again. "I just want to talk for a minute."

"Come back tomorrow." The man shoved against him.

He shook his head. "Only a minute, mister. That's all I'm asking you."

The man sighed. He didn't ease his pressure against the door, but he said, "What'd you want to know?"

"About land in Clear Creek Valley."

"Huh?" For a moment the land agent frowned at him.

Then he stepped back, opening the door. "You thinking of homesteading up *there?*"

"Yeah."

He looked Eben down critically. His eyes lingered on the rifle slung over Eben's shoulder, then returned to his face. "There've been others tried to settle in that valley."

"I know. I been staying up there awhile. I run into that rancher already."

"And you mean to settle there?"

He nodded.

"All right," the man said, but there was a doubtful tinge to his voice. He went to a rack and pulled down a map. Spreading it open, he asked, "You know what quarter section you want to register on?"

"Next to Jacob Hawkins' hold." Eben looked at the map, trying to make sense of the marks and squiggles on it. He picked out what he took to be Jake's spring. Poking a finger at it, he said, "I think this is the place."

"That's been filed on. Just yesterday."

"Huh? Ain't that the spring comes out of the rocks on the slope? Piece of land—" He paused, hunting through his pocket for the paper Alice had given him. He found it and thumbed it open. Setting it on top of the map, he pressed down the creases. "This is the registration for Jake's hold. I'm Jake's brother. I want the land next to his."

"Land next to this piece is open," the agent told him. "But this doesn't belong to Jake Hawkins. The man who's settling there is—" Flipping open a book, running a finger along a page, the agent found a name. "Joe Stoneman."

"That's a damned lie!"

"Hold on, mister! You watch what you're saying!" He isn't a big man, but he looked up at Eben with a

116

hard, ornery scowl.

Catching at his anger, Eben eased back. "Maybe you'd better explain me what you're talking about. This paper Jake's widow give me says he registered for that land last fall."

"He did, but according to my information he died last winter and no one's lived on the land or worked to improve it since. His claim on it's been voided. This Stoneman has put in to take it. He's got the valid claim now."

"Like hell! *I* been working on that land. I been building a cabin and doing my damnedest to get a crop in. I been doing it for Miz Hawkins, to hold her claim."

The agent frowned. "Well, if that's so, you should have come in here and told me. It's too late now. I've already voided Hawkins' claim and entered for this—"

"Like hell you have!" Eben's left hand wrapped into the front of the agent's shirt. His right rose, fisted.

The agent tried to jerk back. Cloth tore under Eben's fingers. Stumbling, the agent fell against the desk. He grunted, grabbing at its edge. Shadows flickered wildly as the lamp behind him tottered.

Eben saw it. Automatically, he started to grab for it. Ducking, the agent bumped his arm. His knuckles brushed the chimney as the lamp toppled.

Oil spattered out of the well, taking flame as it spread. Fire leaped over the papers on the table.

Cursing, the agent slapped at it with his hands.

Eben dropped the rifle and snatched off his coat. He flung it over the flames. The room went twilight dark.

Still muttering curses, the agent opened a drawer and brought out a candle. As he lit it, Eben peeled up the coat. Edges of the cloth were charred, but not as bad as the papers. Some of them weren't much more than crushed black ash.

The hand that held the candle trembled with rage. The agent snarled at Eben, "Goddamn you! I wouldn't register you a claim if you were the president of the United States! I wouldn't—"

Eben wheeled as the door slammed open. He recognized the man who rushed in. At the same instant, he read recognition in the man's eyes on him.

"What the devil's happening here?" the marshal snapped, stopping just through the doorway. He surveyed the room. Reaching for the pistol on his thigh, he gazed narrow-eyed at Eben. His fingers closed on the butt; ready to draw, as he said, "You're one of the damn tramps I've already run out of this town once."

"Arrest him!" the land agent hollered. "He come in here and started a riot. Set fire to the place. Arrest him!"

"I'll be glad to." Still eying Eben coldly, the lawman lifted his gun and leveled it. "I'll learn you when I run a man out, *I mean it!*"

Eben offered no defense. It wasn't exactly awe that held him silent. But facing the justice, he couldn't find words.

The man told him he was guilty of disturbing the peace. He was given his choice of a ten-dollar fine or a two-week jail sentence. It was a damned hard choice.

That gold eagle in his pocket rightfully belonged to Alice. It wasn't for buying himself out of trouble. It was land money. He couldn't go back to her and tell her she'd lost her holding, he hadn't been able to file a claim of his own, and they were out ten dollars to boot.

But he wasn't sure he could stand two weeks locked in a prison cell either. Not without losing everything he'd gained being free. He'd go crazy in jail . . .

118

Silently cursing, he struggled with his thoughts and told himself two weeks of his time wasn't worth ten dollars of Alice Hawkins' money. He worked up voice enough to answer huskily that he'd go to jail.

It didn't take long for the dark, cramped little hole behind the strap-iron barred door to turn into hell. It crawled and stunk, and it filled up with nightmares that were too damned well remembered. They were far more vivid than the memories of real things.

He tried to cling to images of the valley, to thoughts of daylight and clean breezes and the scents of the woods. But the dark silence overwhelmed him.

He slept fitfully and woke thinking he'd be called out to march in lock step to the shoe shop. It took a while to work away from the feeling and recapture the memories that belonged to now. They were the ones that seemed like the half-forgotten dreams.

The greasy meat and fried beans the marshal brought him did nothing to ease his hunger.

It was the seventh day, by his count, when the door rattled unexpectedly. It swung open, letting the light of a coal oil lamp wash into his face. He pressed his back against the far wall as he blinked against it.

Holding up the lamp, the marshal said, "Come on, Hawkins. You got some company."

It took him a moment to react. Bewildered, he came forward in obedience. The lawman led him into the office.

Beyond the unpainted panes at the top of the window the setting sun was a flame. It sent dusty shafts of light angling into the room, making bright patches on the things it touched. He gazed at one patch on the desk top as he told himself where he was. And who he was.

Defiantly, he lifted his head.

A man sat waiting on the settle across from the desk. He watched Eben oddly. It was the land agent.

Taking a deep breath, swallowing hard, Eben said, "You want to see me?"

The agent nodded.

With a jerk, the marshal opened a deep drawer in the desk. He hefted out a paper sack and dumped its contents on the desk. "Here's your belongings, Hawkins. Sign for 'em and you're free to leave."

"Huh?" Eben stared at the pocket pistol, the box of cartridges, the coins, and odds and ends he'd been carrying. He'd thought it was the seventh day, not the fourteenth. How could he have got that far confused away from the true time?

The marshal nodded toward the land agent. "Mister McCracken, here, had a talk with the justice. Everything's cleared up. You're free to go."

Still not understanding, Eben signed the paper and gathered up his belongings. He was surprised to see that all of his money was still there. As he stuffed things into his pockets, he asked the land agent, "You ain't mad at me now?"

"I've been doing some investigating," McCracken said. His voice seemed apologetic. "If you don't mind, Mister Hawkins, I'd like to buy you a drink and talk about a few things."

Eben started at the idea, almost shying away from it. But he told himself again that he was Eben Hawkins and a free man. And there was business he wanted to tend if the land agent would let him. He nodded. Then he made him self put it into words. "I'd be obliged."

The land agent seemed relieved. "As I said, I've—"

"You'll excuse me, Mister McCracken," Eben interrupted. He rubbed his knuckles against the scruff of beard. He felt filthy, pesk-ridden. He couldn't stand it much longer. "You'll excuse me, but I *got* to get cleaned up first."

"Hawkins," the marshal put in. "Twice you've come into this town and quick as you got here, you got into trouble. Right now you've got money and I don't have a charge against you, so that gives you the right to come and go as you please. But you start something in this town once more—" He let it hang in silent threat.

Eben wanted to protest. He wanted to explain that he hadn't started it either time. He gazed at the patch of sunlight, hunting words. But he couldn't shape them.

Nodding in discouraged submission, he mumbled, "Yes, sir."

# CHAPTER 10

SHAVED, CLIPPED, AND SCRUBBED, EBEN WALKED out of the barbershop with the rifle slung on his shoulder and his hands jammed into his pockets. He paused to breathe deep of the fresh night air.

Leaving the jail, he'd been bad scared. Now he found that he felt like Eben Hawkins, like a free man, again. He was surprised, and damned pleased, at how quickly he'd managed to recapture that feeling. He savored it. Head high, he strode down the plank walk to meet McCracken.

The land agent led him onto a side street to a saloon that was quieter than the ones fronting on the railroad. They settled at a corner table with a couple of beers, and the agent began to explain.

He started by telling Eben that the land office in Washington was so piled up with claims and complaints and problems over the Homestead Act that they couldn't handle them, so he took it on himself to make as many decisions as he could right here.

He said he was aware of the troubles people had been having when they tried to settle in Clear Creek Valley, but there was nothing he could do about it himself, except paper work. He was anxious to see the rancher's hold on the valley broken, though.

"After that fracas with you, I asked a few questions," he continued. "The answers I got decided me to take a trip over to Garrison for myself I talked to some people there. Talked to Missus Hawkins . . ."

"You didn't tell her I was in jail?"

He nodded uncomfortably. "She was right upset."

"You shouldn't of told her," Eben muttered, hoping she wouldn't think too poorly of him for it.

"She said that you intended to work the holding in the valley, regardless of Starrett's threats. A man who'd done some hunting up that way said he'd seen you had a cabin most built. Another feller'd heard a rumor that Starrett tried to burn it, but you ran him off?"

"Yeah."

"The folks in Garrison think right highly of you."

That surprised him. Nobody there knew him, except Alice. He supposed they were mixing him up with Jake, thinking he'd be like his brother.

"I also found out that this Stoneman who's filed on the land in question is one of Starrett's hired hands," McCracken went on. "Frankly, I don't have a shred of belief that he intends to settle the land. I think it's just a ruse to keep you off it."

Eben nodded.

"Well, according to the law, a homesteader had to be living on his land and improving it within six months after he's registered if he wants to prove out and get a clear title."

"You mean if Stoneman ain't actually settled there in six months, I can take it up again?"

"That's right."

"But six months—it'll be winter then. I won't be able to do anything. I won't be able to start a crop or make improvements until next spring. Almost a year—"

"I've been giving it some thought," the agent told him. "If you're really anxious to settle there and you really mean to keep the holding, I might be able to help you gain back that time."

"How?"

"It seems to be that a busy man like me just might make a mistake and accidentally enter two different claims for the same piece of land. If that were to happen, whichever man had actually settled and improved the land, *he'd* be the one with the valid claim. If you want to file on it right now . . ."

"He couldn't call the law to run me off, on account he had first claim?"

"There isn't much law around here, especially not outside the town limits. He'd have to bring in a U. S. marshal. He'd have to say that he'd meant to settle the land himself but you'd kept him from it. I don't think Starrett would care to have a Federal officer investigating his hired hand's intent in this matter. And if he tried complaining to me," McCracken grinned slyly, "I'd simply pass the problem along to Washington. They might get around to it in a year or two. Or three."

Eben studied on the idea. "It'd be five years from now that I'd finish proving out and get the patent? Not five years from when Jake registered?"

"I'm afraid so," the agent said, nodding. "It's the best I can do for you, unless you've been in the Army."

"Does that help? I've done some soldiering."

"Not for the Confederacy, I hope. No, I don't suppose you're old enough to . . ."

"I was in the war. For the Union."

"Drummer boy?"

"Artilleryman," Eben answered indignantly.

McCracken lifted a brow in surprise. "Long? Better than nine months?"

"I don't s'pose I was in the war all of nine months," Eben owned, wondering if that would count against him in whatever McCracken had in mind. "I got took prisoner."

"Exchanged and mustered out? Would it add up to nine months of service altogether?"

"Exchanged, hell! They give up on exchanging prisoners right about the same time I got took. I was in them damn camps more'n a year!"

"That's great!"

"Huh?"

"I don't—I—" the land agent stammered. "What I'm trying to say is that if you were in the Army more than nine months, all the time that you served can be deducted off the time you have to prove out for your patent on the land."

Incredulous, Eben said, "You mean something good's come out of that damn business?"

"How long from the time you were enlisted until you were mustered out?"

He counted it in his mind. More than seven months of the war, then over a year of prisoner camps, and at least another six months of the hospital. "More'n two years, I s'pose. I got it all on these papers."

"You have them with you?"

"Yeah." He always kept them with him—the papers that said the Army'd had done with him, that the State of Illinois was through with him, and that he was a free man.

"That'll leave you with less than three years to work for your patent," the agent was saying. "It's a lot quicker than you'd have it if you'd been keeping up the claim for your brother's widow."

Eben nodded, wondering how Alice would take all this. He'd left her thinking she owned the land. Now it would be in *his* name. Well, if there was the kind of trouble with Starrett that he expected, she'd be a lot better off that way. And if he proved it out, once the title was clear, he could turn it over to her.

McCracken swallowed down the last of his beer. "Lets us go on over to the office. I'll open up and get your claim registered."

"I'm obliged," Eben said. He knew that the agent was bending regulations to do this, and it puzzled him. Why should a person go to that kind of trouble for somebody else when there was no profit in it for him? Just for the reason McCracken claimed—just to help?

The fees took his gold eagle and some of the small coin. He didn't much mind parting with the money, though, when he got back a paper saying that he, Eben Hawkins, had lawful rights to the land in Clear Creek Valley. He folded the paper with careful respect and put it with the other papers that were so important in his life. He thanked McCracken again before he left the office.

Ambling along the walk, he felt lightheaded, almost feverish. Not in a bad way, though. Not in a sick way but with a happiness. The right to homestead the land was *his*. The papers he held said he had the right to dream and to fight to make the dreams come true.

The next morning, he had time to kill in Cheyenne before the westbound cars came through. He wandered around, browsing in shops, thinking on things he might buy when the farm profited and he had money of his own in his pocket.

He hadn't meant to spend any of the coin he had left now. But on a sudden impulse he laid out fifty cents for a bright green scarf of some filmy stuff to take back to Alice.

As soon as he had it in his pocket and was out of the store, he got the feeling it had been a fool idea.

Riding the blinds back to Garrison, he kept worrying on how he was going to explain to her about the land. He had to make it clear to her that he felt it was still rightfully hers and he intended to treat it that way. He didn't want her thinking he meant to steal it from her.

By the time he reached the lodging house, he had a speech all spelled out in his head for her. When he saw her, though, it went to pieces. And the fuss she made over the scarf just got him worse befuddled. It wasn't a fine enough gift to warrant the pleasure she seemed to take in it.

When he finally managed to struggle out an explanation of what he'd done about the homestead, she didn't seem upset at all. She listened him out patiently, then asked if it was the way he wanted it.

Mustering up all his reasons, he told her it was. When he started to say why, she stopped him of it. She said she'd agree to whatever he thought was best. She insisted on it.

He was feeling mixed up and vaguely guilty when he left her. It just didn't seem right. She should have fought him over it. Then he could have argued back and convinced her.

He pondered a long while before he figured out that it wasn't *her* but himself he wanted to convince. The trust she put on him bothered him. She seemed to have the same faith in him that she must have had in her husband. Only he *wasn't* Jake. And he knew he never could be. He wasn't willing to try.

If she knew him better, he thought, she wouldn't trust him so. If she knew the way he'd almost shriveled up and died In jail, she'd have been as shamed as he felt himself.

From what he knew of his brother, Jake had been strong and competent, able to face anything that came along. His own strength—what there might be of it— was in Clear Creek Valley. The one thing he felt competent at was farming. He was anxious to be away from the town that overwhelmed him and back at the farm.

Picking up a few supplies, he headed out. He knew the way well enough now to keep off the ranch road. Afoot, it wasn't hard traveling through the woods and it was more direct. Maybe wiser, too. Several times, he glimpsed riders moving through the forest. They looked like cowboys. He felt certain they were Starrett's men.

None of them seemed to spot him. He kept to the brush, and come nightfall, he bedded in a hidden place among the rocks. In the morning, he covered the signs of his camp and moved on cautiously, the rifle in his hand.

He swung wide through the forest, coming out on the bluff that overlooked Jake's land—*his* land. There was nothing but charred rubble and cold ash where the cabin had stood. The ground he'd begun to plow was churned over as if hoofs had trampled and milled across it.

He wasn't surprised. He'd been gone close to two weeks. In that much time, he hadn't doubted Starrett would check up and find the place with no one to protect it. The rancher and his men would have enjoyed destroying all the work that had been done on it. Eben had expected that.

But knowing beforehand didn't ease the pain of seeing his work in ruins. Running his thumb over the action of the rifle, he gazed at the ashes and battered earth. He wondered if Starrett thought he'd abandoned the hold for good. The rancher might have a notion the whole business was over and done with now.

Well, if he did, he'd find out his mistake.

Scanning the valley, Eben decided more had happened than just the ruin of his farm. The browsing cattle were gone. He recalled Cully saying as how in the spring they were moved to a different range. From the look of things they'd been herded upvalley. Real recent, too.

Giving a shrug to resettle the pack of supplies, he started walking again. He figured to drift up the valley a ways himself and see what was to be seen.

By twilight, he still hadn't found anything except the trampled swath the herd had traveled. But as he settled to open himself an airtight, he spotted faint traces of smoke rising in the distance. He ate quickly and hurried on to investigate.

The first of the night darkness made traveling slow. But when the moon rose, it was almost full. It spilled a fair bit of light into the valley. He moved faster then, though he kept to the shadowy edges of the woods. There was no way of knowing what he'd find up ahead.

Before he saw anything, he caught the scents of cattle and lingering hints of the cookfire. A camp, he thought.

Maybe with pickets on guard. He worked up the slope a ways, moving cautiously.

As he climbed a low ridge, he heard the shuffling of hoofs, deep-drawn breathing, and hearty snoring. Then he saw the herd.

It was a sea of cattle settled into the valley. Most of them were lying down, shadowy lumps catching the glint of moonlight on the tips of their horns. An impressive sight. It must really be something to see them all moving, he thought. Probably a real job of work to keep them going, all together and in the right direction.

He wondered how far they traveled in a day and how many men there were to handle them. It seemed likely that a cowboy really earned his wage, doing work like that.

A couple of horsemen were riding slowly around the edges of the herd. From the look of things, they were the only guards. He hadn't found a trace of pickets in the woods. But then, unless the cowboys expected trouble from outside, they wouldn't have any reason to post them.

He supposed they weren't expecting him.

The men were camped upslope a ways from the herd. He could see them wrapped in rumpled blankets on the ground around a canvas-topped wagon. Beyond them, he could make out a good few horses bunched up together as if they were penned.

Working his way along the backside of the ridge, he got in fairly close above the camp. He stretched out on his belly to study it.

Those riders guarding the herd seemed to be the only ones awake. And from the way they were riding, they looked close to drowsing. The horses moved slowly, as if by habit. The men slumped in their saddles. It was all very peaceful and quiet.

He felt a small twinge of sorrow at the idea of disturbing it. The cowboys weren't personally to blame for the argument between Starrett and himself. But then soldiers weren't always to blame for starting the wars they fought in. It was the soldiers, though, who got hurt or killed or were penned up to starve or die of ugly sicknesses.

These long-horned Texas cattle were strange to him. He didn't know much about their temperament, though they acted like wild animals when they were out grazing on the range. What he'd seen of western horses, they were mostly half-wild and quick to run. The bunch he'd loosed from those pens at the winter quarters had sure lit out like the devil was on their tails. If those horses down by the camp were to get scared and take off in a rabble retreat, he wondered if the cattle would join them. It seemed likely. But even if they didn't, it would stir things up a mite to have the horses light out.

There wasn't anything between him and the camp except open ground. He was afraid he couldn't get very close without some of the patrolling riders spotting him. He sure didn't want that happening. It might be a chance he'd have to take, though.

He squirmed out a short ways on his belly, hoping to get a better look at the horses. There were several on a picket line. The rest seemed to be held by nothing more than a rope stretched out for a pen. He didn't think that would do much to hold them if they took a notion to run. The problem was how to give them such a notion. It had to be something more certain than a flung rock or even a rifle shot. He figured he wouldn't get but one chance.

A cannon and spherical case would have done it nicely. He recollected shells bursting behind enemy lines sending cavalry horses into wild panic. But he lacked for the gun and ammunition both. Wondering what he might have that would do the job, he started crawling back to cover.

As he twisted, he felt the lump in his coat pocket. It was that little cap-and-ball pistol. Nestling behind the line of the ridge, he drew it out thoughtfully. There was a box with a couple of dozen or more cartridges for it in his other pocket.

After a moment of study, he pulled the turkey-red kerchief from his hip pocket and held it in the moonlight. Up close, he could make out the bits of white in the print, but at a distance he likely wouldn't be able to see it at all. He'd need something brighter, something solid white. Or maybe—

Digging into the pack of supplies, he came up with an airtight. He ripped off the label and held the tin can out at arm's length. The metal glimmered in the pale light.

He grinned to himself as he cut open the top, then gulped down the tomatoes. When it was empty, he pushed his kerchief into it for a lining. Biting open the paper cartridges, he began to dump the powder from them into it.

There were twenty-six cartridges in the box. That should be enough without having to work the loads out of the pistol. He figured it at around thirteen drams of powder. And about thirty percussion caps. He put them in with the powder, knotted the corners of the kerchief, and stuffed them down into the can.

It had to have more heft if he meant to throw it far. No need to waste good lead for that, though. Pocketing the slugs he'd taken out of the cartridges, he located a few bits of rock with his fingers. He put them gently into the can, then added a fistful of dirt and grass to finish out the packing. When the can was snugly full, he thumbed the cut edges closed. As he got to his feet with it, he unslung the rifle and leaned it ready at his side.

Still grinning, he flung the can toward the horses.

The jar of falling on the grassy earth wasn't enough to set off the caps. He hadn't expected it to be. The can hit ground and bounced, flashing in the moonlight.

He heard a startled horse snort, and was aware of one of the riders wheeling to see what was the matter. But he didn't take his eyes off the glint of metal where the airtight had landed.

Lifting the rifle, he sighted carefully and fired.

Dirt jumped about a handspan away from the can. Suddenly wakened men grunted and hollered in surprise. Horses shuffled nervously. Cattle moaned and began to rise to their knees.

Gently, he triggered a second shot.

The sheen of tin turned into a brilliant orange flare. Sparks and burning tatters of cloth showered in the sharp snap of the blast.

Dropping flat to the earth, Eben blinked against the image of the explosion that was still in his eyes. Over the thin ringing in his ears, he heard a rumbling thunder beginning to grow. It rose to roll over the shouts of the cowboys, almost drowning them out.

Curious, he propped up on his elbows and looked over the top of the ridge.

It was all hell broke loose in the bottoms. Horses and cattle were running crazy. Men raced back and forth, some barefoot, some with shirttails flapping in the moonlight. They grabbed for horses that were determined not to be caught. Frantic animals plunged past them. The bulk of the herd was bolting upvalley. The few men on horseback scrambled after them. It was awesome to see the herd running that way, the great mass of cattle like a river just broke through a dam, surging through the valley. And the men trying desperately to control them. He wondered if it was possible for anything to stop them until they were of a mind to do it themselves.

One of the nearby cowboys caught a horse. As he swung onto it, he began to bellow *Bringing in the Sheaves*. It was as loud as he could holler, but it had a long and mournful sound to it. The tune lingered in Eben's mind after the sound was lost under the clamor.

The enemy was routed, he thought, watching with satisfaction. It was wilder than an upturned ant heap. And in all the confusion, no one seemed to be thinking of the source of the trouble. At least nobody was heading up this way.

Grinning to himself, he shouldered the rifle and started downvalley. He'd stirred up a nice piece of hell back there. Starrett should be able to figure out easy enough who had caused it. And why.

# CHAPTER 11

EBEN WAS SURE THERE'D BE COMPANY SHOWING UP AT the homestead sooner or later. Likely as soon as they could make it. Right now there was probably someone hunting for the place he'd fired the rifle from. Maybe looking to trail him from there. He wondered if Starrett had dogs that could track. Well, he'd managed to keep ahead of a pack of hounds back in the damned Georgia swamps, even though he'd been fevered at the time. He figured he could do at least as well with anything Starrett put on his heels now.

There were plenty of small streams in the slopes, all feeding into Clear Creek like lanes into a highway. He kept to rocky ground till he came to one. Pulling off his boots, he stepped into it. The water was cold, but it ran fast and wouldn't hold a footprint or a scent.

He stayed in the water wherever he could until his feet were numb with the cold. Then he hunted up a spot of bare rock to come out on. Wearing his boots again, he clambered up to the high land.

Dawn was rising when he finally got to the place he had in mind. It was a wooded crag on the far side of the valley, overlooking the farm and the scarp behind it.

Weary and footsore, he settled in the brush beside a fallen tree trunk. Laying his arm along the log, he rested his head against it and fell asleep.

He wasn't sure what woke him. He didn't think he'd heard the horses from where he was. They were a good ways down the valley. About a dozen riders bunched up together out of easy rifle range of the scarp where he'd hidden last time Starrett had come calling. He couldn't make out their faces, but he recognized the rancher's wiry figure.

He sat up and crossed his arms over his knees. Resting his chin on them, he watched curiously.

Starrett pushed his horse forward a couple of steps. Cupping his hands to his mouth, he gave a holler. Eben could hear the call, though the words were indistinct. It looked like Starrett figured he was holed up on the scarp again and was trying to talk him into coming down and bargaining. He wondered if the man really thought he'd do it. What kind of a fool did Starrett take him for?

Something was moving on the scarp. Squinting, he

saw it. A man afoot was working his way across the rock face from above, angling toward the ledge. And he was carrying a rifle.

It all came clear. Starrett wasn't here to bargain. He was baiting a trap. He was sure Eben would be hiding on the same perch, so he and his riders were there to hold his attention while a sharpshooter crawled into position to get a clear shot at him.

He grinned, thinking as how the poor bastard would be right surprised when he got there after all that hard climbing and discovered the trap was empty. Starrett would likely be fair disappointed. He wished he had a sharp pair of field glasses so he could see the rancher's face when he got the news.

The sharpshooter wasn't having any easy time of it. He clung to the rock, feeling cautiously for each foothold. He moved slowly and hesitantly from one to another. All the while, Starrett kept hollering and cajoling. He seemed to be bothered a mite by not getting any sort of answer. And he sounded like he was wearing the skin out of his throat.

The sharpshooter moved with effort that had Eben tense in sympathy. The man dragged himself onto a small outjut of rock, knelt there, and wiped at his face. Then he poked his head out.

He started visibly. Uncertain, he scanned the rocks above and below him. He looked toward the ledge again as if he couldn't really believe it was empty.

After a while of considering, he clambered to his feet. Bracing one hand on the rock, he waved the other and shouted to Starrett.

Eben could hear the hoarse-voiced boiling curses the rancher answered with. He pitied the poor man who'd failed to find the quarry. Starrett sounded mad enough to shiver mountains with his hollering and to tear them out at the roots with his bare hands. He'd sure spill all that bile over onto somebody. And since Eben wasn't to be found, the sharpshooter seemed to be next in line for it.

Using his mount viciously, Starrett galloped up to the ashes of the cabin. He forced the animal into the rubble, jerking at its mouth when it hesitated to step over tumbled logs. He seemed upset that everything was already ruined so there was nothing he could do now to add to the destruction.

The whole crew galloped back and forth a bit, using up the energy they'd have stored for this venture. At last they gave it up and headed out, riding hard and fast. Once they were out of sight, Eben dug into his supplies for breakfast, then stretched out, and dropped into a deep, satisfied sleep.

He woke feeling as if he might be catching a cold, and that worried him some. He could be in real trouble if he took feverish out here alone. But in a few days the cold wore away without ever turning bad. He kept his camp on the crag for a week, watching over the farm.

There were two more visits from Starrett's men. The first time, about half a dozen riders crept in along the edges of the forest by twilight. They kept watch all through the night and the next day, working hard to stay out of sight. Late the next afternoon, they drifted out to inspect the ground and the ashes. Eben knew they wouldn't find sign of anyone being there since Starrett tried the sharpshooter trick. Obviously disappointed, they rode off.

A day later a lone man came in cautiously. He made a circuit of the place, then headed back upvalley. At the distance, Eben hadn't been sure, but he thought it was his own lineback dun the man was riding.

He kept his watch a few more days, but the supplies began to run low. There was no game to be had on the crag. And he had a notion Starrett was satisfied that he'd left the farm. With the rifle ready in his hand, he headed down toward it.

There were a lot of things to be done before the end of the six months he had to establish his right to the claim. He wanted to get at them.

After the failures, it didn't seem likely Starrett would try more mass attacks. If he found out Eben was back, he'd probably try with another sharpshooter. One who'd skulk up through the woods and lie in wait to pick off his quarry like a game animal.

Eben figured his best defense would be good cover close at hand. If a sharpshooter missed the first shot at him, he'd be able to duck for his hole and try shooting back.

He studied the scarp face and the lay of the land. Most of it was open, so it was useless to him for the time being. But across the stream from the cabin site, the rock wall got rougher with a thick scattering of big boulders at its foot. They offered the kind of cover he needed. He'd stick close to them. He'd do his work during the half-light of dawn and dusk, and under the moon when there was enough of it.

He dug out his caches of supplies, moving them to handier places. Then he began the work he'd set for himself.

He had already given up hope of putting in a truck crop this season. The ox was gone again. But even if he'd had it here to plow with, he didn't fancy the idea of trying to work out in the open fields.

He decided instead to put a garden patch up near the

137

rocks. The ground could be broken with a hoe. The crop might be small, but it would serve his own table. Once it was in, he could get on with building another house of some kind.

The days passed as peacefully as he could ask. He finished the garden and began his cabin. This time he built with poles instead of logs, using the stone face of the scarp for a back wall. He tucked the shack in close to the boulders where it was half-hidden from sight.

It wouldn't be much of a cabin, but he figured he could get through the winter in it. And once the time came that he could put up a real house on the land, the shack would make a decent enough outshed.

He had the walls almost shoulder high and was working well into daylight when he spotted a rider.

It was a lone horseman coming downvalley at an easy lope. He rode as if he felt no need or reason to hide himself. He sure wasn't the sharpshooter that Eben had been expecting.

That didn't ease Eben's concern, though. Unslinging the rifle, he ducked into the rocks and set his sights on the bobbing figure.

The rider halted at a distance. Rising in the stirrups, he scanned the homestead. From where he was, Eben figured he should be able to spot a corner of the cabin and part of the garden plot if he looked careful enough.

Braced against the rocks, he followed the rider with the sights as the horse began to move again. It came on at a casual amble.

Suddenly Eben recognized the man he was watching. It was Cully.

He frowned as he held aim on the moving figure. He didn't want to shoot at Cully. The idea bothered him bad. But if Starrett had sent the cowboy—he didn't know what he'd do.

Cully put both hands to the reins, holding them high in front of him. He rode in closer, then stopped again.

"Hawk?" he called.

"I got a gun pointed at you," Eben answered.

"You don't need it. I ain't looking for trouble."

"Swear it?"

"Sure." Cully raised his right hand in the gesture of an oath.

Eben lowered the rifle. Holding it in both hands, he stepped from the rocks. "Come on in."

Cully came. He rode up and sat there on his horse, looking sadly at Eben. "I sure hoped you wasn't back here. Had a fear you might be, though."

"What do you want?"

"I dunno. I just kinda had to find out if you were here or not."

"Starrett didn't send you?"

He shook his head. "I'm just out looking around. Prowling lest we missed any strays in the cow hunt. First chance I've had. We sure been working like hell. You mind I step down?"

"Come on," Eben muttered, still feeling uncertain about the cowboy's presence. He trusted Cully's word, but he didn't like him being here this time. Especially not if he had to report back to his boss what he'd found. "You gonna tell Starrett you seen me?"

"If he asks me, I will. I do what he says, long as I'm working for him."

"Did you help him burn the cabin while I was away?"

He nodded and asked in return, "Hawk, was it you stampeded our beeves one night a ways up from here?"

Eben figured he meant that business with the makeshift bomb. "I s'pose it was."

139

"That's a terrible thing to do!"

"I didn't much like having my cabin burnt."

"But running a herd like that—it taken us all night to get 'em back in hand. It run the tallow right off 'em. It's a terrible thing!" Cully sounded really upset about it.

Feeling vaguely guilty, Eben answered him back, "You with the bunch that come down here looking to kill me the next day?"

"You knew about that?"

"I was watching you."

"The hell! When we couldn't find you then, the old man got a notion you'd finally spooked out. Figured you took one last crack at him by running the beeves and then lit a shuck. The notion didn't pleasure him none, though. You'd already throwed us days behind in our work. He got so ornery that a couple of the boys up and quit on him. That didn't humor him neither. You sure ain't made life no playparty for us." Sighing, he pulled off his hat and wiped his face with his sleeve. Then he stepped into the shade of the rocks and hunkered.

Settling at his side, Eben said, "You see anything of that old red ox that took up with me before?"

"We moved it to summer range 'long with the rest of the beeves. You ain't thinking of taking it back again?"

"I kinda miss it."

"It ain't *your* ox."

"Starrett's using *my* horse, ain't he? I seen one of his men riding it."

Cully gave a reluctant nod in reply.

"Well, I'll call it a fair trade," Eben told him. "My horse for his ox. Sounds fair to me."

"The hell?" he grunted incredulously. "You'd sooner

have an ox than a horse?"

"It'd do me more good. 'sides, that was a right friendly ox. I think he'd get lonesome without anybody to scratch his neck." Eben didn't want to own that he was lonesome, too. But he knew that was a piece of it. The old cow had been company. A time back, he hadn't expected he'd ever long for company. He knew the feeling now, though.

Sighing again, Cully looked at the land. He frowned at the started shack and the garden patch "How long you think you're gonna hold out here?"

"Got a bit over two years to go to get the patent."

"Look, Hawk, you can't lick Starrett. He's got money and fellers working for him, and he's mad enough at you now to kill you on purpose. How the hell you think you can beat him?"

"The way water beats rock." Eben pointed to the deep cut the spring stream had made down the face of the scarp. "I'll just stay at it till the job's done."

"He won't let you!"

Ain't no way he can stop me without he kills me. He ain't gonna have any easy time doing that. Sooner or later one of us will have to either give in or kill the other one. I figure if I can stay alive and stick at it, I'll beat him."

"Man can't help but kinda admire it," Cully mumbled. He poked his finger at the dirt, staring at it as if he was studying on it. "Just like some jugheaded bronc what won't be broke. Man knows the animal is damnfool crazy. Still he can't help but kinda admire it."

Eben grinned in embarrassment.

Looking sideways at him, Cully said, "I sure wish you'd put yourself to something you stood a chance of winning at."

141

"I'll win at this."

The cowboy got to his feet. He kicked at a clod. With his hands jammed into his hip pockets, he gazed off into the distance. Without turning, he said, "Hawk, you gotta be careful. That Jasper feller is still working with us. He's got a mind for killing. He's been asking the boss wouldn't he like you hunted up and got rid of, no matter where you've went off to. If he ever finds out you're the same one as cut that hole in him, he won't wait around for no permission."

"You can tell Jasper he ain't the first man I put a knife into," Eben said coldly.

Cully looked back over his shoulder at him. "That true?"

It wasn't something he felt like bragging on. But it might serve a purpose to let the enemy know this much about himself. He nodded. Thinking of the pardon, he added, "I got a paper to prove it."

"A newspaper?"

"Note from the governor of Illinois. Got his name signed to it."

"The hell!" Cully stared at him, shaking his head as if he weren't sure whether or not to believe it. "What'd he give you a paper for?"

"He agreed I'd done a good job of it." There was a touch of iron in Eben's voice.

Still shaking his head, Cully gathered reins. He stepped up onto his horse, then looked at Eben again. "I dunno. You almost set me to wondering maybe you *can* beat Starrett. I don't see no way of it, though."

"Like water on rock."

"I dunno," he muttered as he gigged the horse.

Eben felt oddly sad, as if he'd lost something, as he watched the cowboy ride away.

It was a few days later that the old red ox came drifting downvalley. As he welcomed it home, Eben realized that someone must have intentionally moved it off the summer range and headed it this way. That someone had to have been Cully.

He wondered if the cowboy would ever come calling friendly again, or if the next time they met, it would be from opposite sides of the line.

Since he'd given up the notion of plowing or putting in a heavy cabin this season, he lacked work for the ox. But he wanted it around anyway. He fed it and petted it, and it stayed, nosing into things and making a pest of itself. He had to put up a pole fence to keep it out of the garden patch. And more than once he woke thinking someone was sneaking up on him when it was only the ox. Even so, he was glad for its company.

"You know, old cow, I got half a mind to go into town," he told it one bright warm morning. He owned that it wouldn't understand, but a man had an urge to talk out loud at something now and then. At least the ox would turn its ears toward him and eye him when he did it.

"I really ought to go in and let Miz Alice know how things are coming along. Ought to tell her how I got a cabin up and put in a garden."

Since the ox just chawed as its cud, he answered himself. "Other hand, it's only a pole shanty and a little patch. Not like I had a sound cabin and a decent truck crop planted. Might be she wouldn't think so much of it as I do."

He leaned his arms lazily on the steer's back, looking at the valley as he thought about the girl. She'd been in his mind a lot lately. He wanted her to share his pride in the farm. He realized it would hurt him deep if she didn't, but he longed to see her again, no matter what. He was willing to face the unpleasantness of the town, the walls, the stink of men. He'd be willing to face even worse, if he had to. He sure wanted to see her.

Could leave out first thing in the morning, he told himself. Likely Starrett didn't know he was still around. It d be safe enough to leave the place untended for a few days . . .

Something startled him. He cocked his head, frowning as he listened. There were noises in the woods. A crashing like a bear or elk gone mad. It was heading his way. Unslinging the rifle, he stepped back toward the boulders.

A horseman broke suddenly into the open.

Eben ducked for cover. He watched the rider dash a ways into the valley, then jerk rein, bringing his horse into a rear.

Waving his hat wildly, the man shouted, "Hawkins?"

Eben didn't like the look of it. Taking a brace against the rock, he aimed carefully and squeezed the trigger.

The hat flew out of the rider's hand. For a moment he seemed too shocked to react. Then he screamed, "Don't shoot, for Gawd's sake! Hawkins, hear me!"

"I'm listening," Eben called back.

The horse danced nervously, but the man held a taut rein on it. A desperate urgency honed his voice. "It's your sister-in-law, Hawkins!"

Icy apprehension raced down Eben's spine. He shouted, "What about her?"

"She's hurt."

"What?" He felt a knot twist and jump in his gut. The rifle trembled in his hands. If this was Starrett's doing—

"She's hurt," the man repeated. "She was coming to see you. Accident—her horse—up the road a ways. She's asking for you, Hawkins!"

Scrambling down the rocks, Eben raced toward him. The frantic words had shoved away every other thought. If she was hurt, he had to get to her.

The rider lifted rein, ambling the horse toward him.

Suddenly he knew something was wrong. Jerking to a stop, he heard the sounds of hoofs behind him. His hands knotted into fists as he wheeled.

Two more men were riding toward him. They swung apart, meaning to cut him off from the rocks and the nearest point of woods. The first rider had tricked him into the open. Now the others blocked him from getting to cover again. And he'd dropped the rifle as he'd dashed down from the rocks.

Turning, he glimpsed the first man's grin. He lunged. He meant to grab the rider's leg and unseat him, maybe get hold of the horse. But at a flick of the reins, the animal spun on its haunches. His hands caught only air.

And the others were closing fast behind him.

He started to turn again. He saw a loop rolling down the rope that snaked toward him. Reflexively, he flung up his left hand to fend it off.

It snapped tight, grabbing him by the neck, jerking his hand up to his throat. For an instant he was leaning against it. Then he was on his face in the grass with the rope burning into his flesh. It jammed his wrist hard against his windpipe.

He flailed his free hand wildly, trying to grab at the rope and ease it. But he was flung, dragged, battered at the end of it. Gasping futilely, he felt his lungs cramping. He slid, twisting, over the grass. A red haze was swelling inside his head, blinding him It pounded in his ears. And it became a darkness that was swallowing him.

"Hey! Hey, Hawkins, come on! You ain't dead!"

The voice cut knife-sharp through the darkness. He felt it pierce through his ears into his skull. And something gripped into his hair, shaking his head.

Painfully, his lungs sucked air. It rasped through his throat, wrenching him into a spasm of coughing.

He heard laughter.

He became aware that he was lying on his belly. Whatever held his hair had his head twisted around. He forced open his eyes. As he squinted at the blur he saw, it became a face. The grinning face of the man called Jasper.

Eben closed his eyes again.

A hand slapped hard against his cheek. Jasper demanded, "Come on, Hawkins, look at me."

He obeyed. He looked at the man who hunkered at his side, clutching him by the hair. Past Jasper, he recognized the cowboy called Pete astride a horse. The rope stretched from the saddle horn to the loop that still held his wrist tight against his throat. There was barely enough slack to let him draw breath. He knew that with a touch, Pete could back the horse, jerking the noose closed again.

"Remember me, Hawkins?" Jasper said. "Remember Cheyenne, jailbird?'

"What the hell you doing?" Pete called impatiently.

Jasper looked back over his shoulder. "Having a little fun."

"I don't like it," Pete muttered gruffly.

Rising, Jasper turned toward him. "I don't give a damn whether you like it or not."

The man who'd baited the trap moved into Eben's

range of vision. He nudged his horse up next to Pete's as he said, "Let's get this over with."

"Dammit, I got business with him," Jasper insisted.

"What kind of business?" Pete asked.

Feeling had begun to come back to Eben, and with it, pain. He discovered he was lying on his free hand. Cautiously, he braced and tried moving it. He slid it slowly from under his body.

The men were intent on their talk. They weren't paying any attention to him. He slid the hand up his hip. His fingers touched the sheath on his belt. He edged them along it. They found the hilt of the knife.

A quick move would attract their eyes. And he wasn't sure his aching muscles could move quickly, anyway. He eased the hand to his side again, with the knife in it.

Jasper was gesturing violently as he described having been stabbed. He made it sound like he'd been attacked outnumbered, and unmercifully slaughtered.

Drawing slow breaths, fighting against the fit of coughing that wanted to rise in his throat, Eben snaked his hand along the ground. The knife blade was honed sharp. If he could get it onto the damned rope, he could slash through and—

Jasper wheeled. Laughing gleefully, he slammed out a foot.

The boot heel smashed down onto Eben's hand.

For an instant there was no pain. He felt the crushing of bone. He heard the grating of it as the boot ground his knuckles onto the hard handle of the knife. He was aware of Pete's startled gasp.

Then the pain burst in his hand like an exploding bomb, sending its hot shards tearing through his arm. His body jerked against it, trying desperately to pull away from it.

Jasper howled with delight.

"For Gawd's sake, stop that!" Pete hollered.

Standing heavily on Eben's hand, Jasper looked at him and snapped back, "Hell, whadda you care?"

"The boss just said to get rid of him. You don't have to do nothing like *that* to him," he protested. Flicking reins, he moved the horse forward a short step. It eased the rope slightly.

Through the blur of pain, Eben was aware of the slack. He tried to pry with the wrist that was held against his throat, he felt the rope slip a bit. The breaths came a little easier.

"He owes me!" Jasper was saying angrily. "G'damn him, he'll pay me for sticking that knife into me."

"Not that way."

"Pete's right," the third man put in.

Jasper stepped off Eben's hand and strode toward the horsemen. "The boss told *me* to get rid of him. I'll do it any g'damn way I want! You understand?"

The rope dug into flesh it had already burnt raw on Eben's neck. He pushed his arm against it with all the strength he could muster. It slipped slightly and stopped. He tried again. At last it was up across his palm instead of his wrist. With a painful tug, he jerked the hand free. But he couldn't pull the noose open far enough to work it over his jaw.

He felt with a certainty that he'd die here and now. He didn't want to die alone.

The knife was still in his crushed hand. Lurching to his knees, he grabbed for it.

Pete's horse jerked back, throwing its weight against the rope, hauling him down. It was dragging him back into the red-hazed darkness.

"Ho!" Pete hollered.

The rope eased. Eben gasped for air as he tried to struggle out of the darkness. But something rammed hard into his ribs, driving the breath out of him. He knew it was Jasper's boot.

And he knew he'd managed to grasp the knife in his good hand. Desperately, he tried to swing it.

Jasper kicked again.

Eben felt the blade strike and glance. At best he'd only sliced leather, not flesh. He could hear Jasper's braying laugh.

Fighting the pain and darkness, he tried to roll away from the boot that lashed into his side again. But he knew he couldn't escape it.

"G'dammit!" Pete shouted.

Lightning struck.

Eben heard the blast of it. He felt it hit. It jarred into him, jolting his whole body. The blinding flare of it drove away the pain—drove away all sensation. It broke him loose of the body and flung him into dark, starless night.

He'd been shot, he thought. Killed? There was no sight, no feeling. But, oddly, there was sound. It seemed to be coming from some far distance in thin-strung threads.

"What'd you do that for?" Jasper's voice whined.

"Put him out of his g'damned misery," Pete answered harshly. "You get the hell on your horse and come on, or I'll do the same for you."

"I don't think you shoulda done that, Pete." The third man sounded awed and unhappy. "That was murder."

"What the devil you think the boss sent us to do?" Pete snapped back at him. "Let's get the hell away from here!"

The sounds grew thinner. As they faded, Eben knew

that the last shreds of awareness were slipping away from him. He felt a damned bitter disappointment. And then there was nothing.

# CHAPTER 12

HE HAD BEEN DREAMING. AS HE REALIZED THAT, EBEN told himself that he wasn't dead. But the memory of dying was starkly vivid. He lay motionless in darkness, pondering it. There'd been times he could recall when dreams mixed themselves in with the things that were real until he hadn't been sure which was which. Fever dreams.

He thought he might have been feverish again, but he wasn't certain. His sense of being—his awareness of his body—seemed thin and fine-drawn, ready to snap away from him.

Carefully he gathered broken pieces of memory, trying to sort the real ones from the dreams. Recollections of the valley, the homestead, Alice Hawkins, and the rancher named Starrett seemed real, but he wasn't sure. Maybe he'd waken to discover he was in the Andersonville camp, sick and hungry. Or in the black and airless cell where there'd been nothing except memories.

He knew that the only way to find out would be to finish waking up. He was afraid of that—afraid of the truth he might find. There wasn't any other way, though.

*I am Eben Hawkins,* he told himself as he forced away the filmy dregs of sleep and cautiously opened his eyes.

Awake, he knew that much was true. He was Eben Hawkins. And he was alive. But where? And when?

He discovered that he was lying on a feather bed in a dusky warm light that seemed to filter through closed window blinds. He was in a room with a whitewashed ceiling. The planks overhead were blurred, but he could make them out. And he could hear steady soft sounds, like slow-drawn breathing.

When he tried to turn his head, he found that his neck was sore, inside and out. Almost too stiff to move. He felt raw, painfully sensitive, not just in his body, but his whole being.

From the corner of his eye, he could glimpse someone sitting beside the bed. The chair was cocked back against the wall, and the man's head lobbed to one side as if he were asleep.

Eben forced his neck to turn a little farther. Blinking, he brought the man's face into focus. It was Cully. Puzzled, he studied on that awhile.

When he tried to speak, his voice came hoarsely, without much sound to it. "Cully?"

"Huh?" The cowboy wakened with a start. The chair's front legs hit the floor hard, shattering the stillness. Eben flinched at the sharpness of the sound.

Cully leaned forward, peering at him. "You 'wake?"

"Uh huh." It wasn't easy to try talking. His chest felt cramped up tight, and there was a lump of pain in it. He forced out the words. "Am I Starrett's prisoner?"

"Naw, you're home."

But he didn't have a home. It didn't make sense. He asked, "Where?"

"Lodging house in Garrison."

"How I get here?"

"I drug you in," Cully mumbled, as if he felt

embarrassed by it.

That didn't make sense either. Eben said, "But you work for Starrett?"

"Not any more I don't!"

Another memory crowded in on him. "Alice? She's all right? Not hurt?"

"No. Where'd you get a notion like that?"

"Ways back," he whispered, letting his eyes close again. He felt too tired to go on talking. The effort was making the pain worse. It stirred a nausea in him. There were more things he wanted to know, but he couldn't hold onto them. Even Cully's voice seemed to be growing faint.

"You all right?"

"Yeah. Just tired," he managed to answer.

"Want anything?"

"No."

"Maybe you'd better go back to sleep."

He agreed to that. He knew as he heard Cully say it that he was already beginning to drowse.

When he wakened again, he knew where he was and which were the dreams. Opening his eyes, he found the half-darkness of a low-turned lamp.

It was Alice who sat beside the bed. The lamp was on the table next to her, and she bent close to hold a piece of needlework in its glow. He watched from the corner of his eye, admiring the way her fingers flicked at the work, catching sparks of light on the needle. There was a pleasure in lying silent, just looking at her.

He had a vague feeling that he knew the touch of those hands, not just holding his, but against his face. They'd been gentle, soothing in their touch. He thought it must have been a dream.

It took her a long while to realize that he was awake.

She looked up suddenly, speaking his name softly in surprise.

He grinned at her, feeling oddly shy and embarrassed.

Setting down the needlework, she rose and reached out. Her hand pressed against his forehead, the palm pleasantly cool.

"Fever?" he asked. The thought of it still frightened him. He'd known too much about fever back in Andersonville.

"It's broken now. Almost gone," she said. She smiled at him. But there was a weariness and strain in the set of her face. She'd been worried, he thought.

He had a notion she and Cully had been keeping watch over him and tending him, maybe for a long time. She shouldn't have troubled herself that way. He'd wanted to help her, not to become a worry for her. Huskily, he said, "Sorry—tricked like a damn fool—"

"Shush, don't try to talk. You're still very weak."

He knew that well enough. He was having a hard time keeping his eyes open. Thoughts were trying to slide away from him. But he wanted to apologize for the trouble he'd caused her.

"You shouldn't—I—" He groped for words. She tried to shush him, but he persisted. "I—I'm all right. Don't need to be watched over."

"I *want* to watch over you," she said, still smiling.

There was a strange warmth in her voice, a quality that bewildered him. It stopped him of protesting any more.

She brushed back the hair that straggled on his forehead. Her fingertips traced lightly along the point of his cheek. The touch left its image, like fine, faint sparks playing over his skin,

"Don't worry about anything, Eben," she whispered.

"Everything will be all right."

He didn't want to fall asleep again. Not right now. But he couldn't help it. The world was misting into dreams. Good dreams. Her face and the feel of her hand lingered in them.

The next time he came awake, he found that the vague sense of fuzziness and the raw feel of the pain were gone. He was clearly and completely awake, enough to take stock of himself.

His right arm wouldn't move. It felt as if it was tied across his chest. When he tried to shift it, a shock of pain cut through it.

Groping with his left hand under the coverlid, he found the arm with his fingers. From the elbow down, all he could feel was a thick bulk of bandaging.

He remembered Jasper's boot slamming down on his knuckles. He remembered the sound—the feel—of bone grating on bone. And suddenly there was a godawful fearsome thought overwhelming him. He used his left hand to jerk back the coverlid.

"Hey! What you doing!" Cully'd been slumped in the chair, seeming asleep again. But as Eben moved, he straightened up and scowled sharply, "You ain't trying to get up?"

"No," Eben grunted, pressing his chin down into his chest. He had a shirt on, but the right sleeve was opened up the seam. He gazed at the shapeless lump of muslin that swathed his arm almost to the elbow. "I still got a hand under all that?"

"Reckon you have," Cully said with a hesitancy he didn't like at all. He had too many recollections of battlefield surgery.

"You sure?"

"I dunno," the cowboy owned "Doc kinda fitted the

pieces all back together, but he couldn't promise it'd grow back as good as it was before."

Slowly Eben pulled the coverlid up again. Cully was watching him sideways, waiting for a reaction. He hauled his thoughts together and tried to work some strength into his voice. "That bastard shoulda stomped on my head. For all I been using it lately, I could do without it easy enough."

The solemn uncertainty faded out of Cully's face. He grinned.

"I guess my hand was pretty busted up," Eben said.

"Doc wanted to take it off," the cowboy told him. "Only Miz Alice, she wouldn't let him. She said she coulda got the horse doctor from the stable to do bone-sawing. Said she'd brought Doc here from Cheyenne to patch you up, not take you apart."

"Getting took apart once is enough. How bad was I hurt?"

Cully pursed his lips thoughtfully. "Well now, you'd shed some skin and was scraped and bruised and rope-burnt a mite, and you had some busted ribs and that mashed hand, and there was a pistol ball between your lights and your gizzard, and you'd spilt nigh enough blood to paint a barn. Except for that, you wasn't hurt none at all that I could see."

Eben grinned at him, then asked, "Cully, what are you doing *here*?"

"Got nothing better to do. Like the vittles here. That Miz Alice is one fine cook."

"You quit Starrett?"

"Yeah." He sighed. "It ain't that I got anything against killing a man as needs it bad, or one that's trying hard to kill you back. But the way them fellers put about killing you, I don't hold with that none at all."

155

"How'd you come to find me?"

"Heard it was Jasper the boss had sent to get rid of you. Knew he wouldn't be decent about it. I lit out after 'em. Hoped I could beat 'em to you and warn you they was coming. Only I reckon I wasn't exactly in time."

"I'll allow I could have done with you getting there a mite earlier."

"You sure couldn'ta done with me getting there much later. All I found was the carcass. Figured I'd bury you proper. Got the hole all dug and was ready to shove you in 'fore you give enough of a moan to let me know you wasn't quite ready yet. I damn nigh throwed you in anyway. Hated to waste the hole. Put a lot of work into digging it. Got me a sore back doing it." He laid his hand to his side, grimacing as if he could still feel the terrible pain of it.

"I hate to see a man so bad off," Eben said. "What you need is some of this lying around in bed for a while."

"Depends who with."

"That wouldn't do your sore back no good."

"It'd take my mind off it." Cully grinned. But then the grin faded. He gazed into the distance thoughtfully. "I can see that Jasper mauling a man around the way they done you. And Brady'd likely go along with anything anybody else wanted. But I sure wouldn't of expected it from Pete. He's kinda rough sometimes, but he ain't naturally mean. Not at all."

"Was Jasper's doing," Eben told him. "Pete didn't hold with it. I think it was him that put the bullet in me."

"Pete?"

"Yeah."

"Pete," he said slowly, looking like it troubled him. "Hell. Pete ain't really a bad sort, Hawk. Truth is, he's

156

kinda my friend. I think he wouldn't of done no such thing without the boss had ordered him. You can't hold him all to blame for shooting you. Starrett would of ordered him."

"I ain't much holding it against Pete," Eben answered. "I sure didn't like him dragging me the way he done, but I don't fault him for shooting me. He done me a favor by it."

Cully gaped at him in bewilderment.

"Jasper was treating me damn rough." he explained. "He meant to kill me slow and hard. Pete shot me to stop him of doing me any worse. If he hadn't got right mad about the way Jasper was doing, they might not have left out so quick. Might be they'd have made sure I was dead 'fore they left."

"I'm glad you ain't," Cully said. He sounded relieved. "I'm glad Pete—hell, he ain't a bad sort. It's Jasper. Damn if I understand his kind. Damn if I understand Mister Starrett putting up with him. That old man's sure been getting feisty. You shouldn'ta stampeded his beeves, Hawk. I warned you how he felt about them critters."

"He shouldn'ta burnt my cabin. Don't he know I might feel every bit as strong about that homestead as he does about his damned beeves?"

"I dunno. I reckon I don't understand fellers like you and him. I'd sooner drift ahead of a storm than buck headfirst into the wind."

"I never asked him for nothing that was his," Eben muttered. "All I took was the hundred sixty acres I was entitled to. Government says I got the right."

"He wouldn'ta let you take *one* acre, no matter who says you're entitled. Man like Mister Starrett, he makes his own laws." Cully looked sidways at him. "I tried to tell you that you shouldn't go against him. I tried to warn you that you'd get hurt."

"It ain't your fault."

The cowboy turned away. He walked over to the window and looked out. He seemed really troubled. It bothered Eben. He didn't want to be causing worries for other people.

Thinking of Alice, he asked, "Cully, did you ever collect the wage you were talking about back when we met?"

"What?"

"I mean you got money enough I might could borrow some from you?"

"I reckon I could get hold of enough. How much you need the lend of?"

"Enough to pay whatever this room and my food's costing. I can't let Alice pay it out."

Cully turned to face him again. "It ain't costing anything."

"Huh?"

"Carsons, the folks that run this lodging house, they said it wouldn't cost nothing. Said business was right poor this season, and it didn't look like nobody'd have any use for the room, so they wouldn't be losing nothing by keeping you in it. And since they was having vittles cooked up for the dining room anyhow, it wouldn't matter much to make for one more. They're right nice people, Hawk. They think real high of you."

"I'll pay 'em back," he mumbled.

"They ain't gonna want it. They won't take kindly to it."

"What the hell you mean?"

"There's times folks want to do for a person and they don't want nothing back in pay," Cully said. "Don't you know that?"

"No." It didn't fit much of what he knew about the world. But he had to own he didn't know much about the world. Sometimes it seemed like he knew even less than he'd thought. He eased back into the pillow, studying on it and on the way these people had concerned themselves with him.

After a while, he said, "A man feels debted. He feels bound to pay what he owes."

"Yeah," Cully muttered from some deep thought of his own. " 'Specially for what he does wrong."

He sounded like he meant something in particular, something that troubled him. Eben opened his eyes and looked at him, but the cowboy was standing with his back turned, gazing out the window again.

It was a couple or so weeks later that Cully came in grinning and dumped a fistful of coin and greenbacks on the bedside table. "Well, Hawk," he announced, "we've turned rich."

"What are you talking about?" Eben grunted, eying the heap of money suspiciously.

"You recall a time back when you laid out four bits for me to ride the cars? I said I'd pay you back."

"That looks like more'n any fifty cents to me."

"Little over forty dollars " Cully grinned "Wasn't but fifty cents when I planted her, but oh, how she grew!"

"Money doesn't grow."

"Does when you know how to tend it." He pulled up the chair and settled in it with his feet on the bed rail "'While back, I went over to Cheyenne for some fun. Took along a dollar for the tiger. Bucked him good and come back with five. Second time I went in, I took the five and come back with almost twenty. Went again yesterday and turned twenty into over eighty. Figured I owed you half that dollar I started with, so there she is, 'long with all her young'uns."

"No."

"What you mean *no*?"

"No, I don't want your money."

"It ain't like I'd *worked* for it. I know that game. I know the dealer, and I've found out how it's rigged They taken it away from most the dumb cowboys, but they give it to me."

"It's *your* money."

"It ain't mine. Half of it's rightfully yours. You lent to me, Hawk. You give me of your vittles when I was hungry. I got a right to pay you back."

"You got no right to pay me more'n you took from me," Eben said.

"G'damn you!" Cully snapped, sounding really angry. He swung up out of the chair and strode to the window.

Eben watched him, remembering what he'd said about folks doing for other people without wanting to be paid back. This could be Cully's way of doing, he thought. But the cowboy seemed to have more on his mind than just a charitable gift.

He stood at the window, looking out, with his back to Eben. Huskily, he said, "I took more from you than you know. It was me as told Starrett you'd come back to the valley. That's when he sent Jasper after you. I owe you more'n that damned money, Hawk. Only I don't know no way to pay you."

"You warned me you'd tell him," Eben said slowly. "You told me he was your boss and if he asked you, you'd have to tell him. I s'pose he asked."

"That's the damned truth!" Cully wheeled to face him. "I swear it to God, that's the truth of it! I was sorry

160

for it then. I meant to warn you of it. I walked out on him and headed to warn you, and I'd of fought them with you, only I got there too damned late! I mean it, Hawk!"

"Hell, he'd have heard it from somebody sooner or later," he muttered. The cowboy was looking at him in a desperate, pleading way that made him uncomfortable. He felt as if he had to ease Cully's concern somehow. "Look, if it had been somebody else who told him, maybe nobody'd have come along when you did. Maybe there wouldn't anybody except the buzzards have found me."

It was an idea that obviously hadn't occurred to the cowboy before. He grabbed at it, examining it hopefully. Slowly, he gave Eben a shy, uncertain grin. "Yeah, I reckon that's so, ain't it?'"

"I'm lucky it was you as told him."

"I'm still sorry for it. Damned sorry I wasn't there no sooner."

"Well, it's past now," Eben said.

Cully nodded. He gestured toward the pile of money. "Hawk, it ain't that I'm trying to buy you into forgiving me. It's—hell—it's when a man has more of a thing than he needs himself and there's somebody else can make good use of it. Like you shared of your chicken with me back at Omaha that time."

Eben recalled he'd hardly shared that food willingly. He'd resented every mouthful the others had taken. But as he remembered it, the feeling seemed strange. And wrong.

He looked at the money, understanding what Cully meant, and said, "I'm obliged."

The cowboy's grin broadened. He seemed more than a little embarrassed. Turning away, he gazed out the window again.

Eben felt embarrassed himself. The rapping at the door came as a relief to him. Cully opened it, and Alice walked into the room, carrying a covered tray. The cowboy muttered something and left. She came on over to set the tray on the table beside the bed.

"What you got there?" Eben asked. Bracing with his good hand, he dragged himself to sitting up. It was getting easier every day. He had a notion he'd be on his feet pretty soon, regardless of whether the others agreed with him.

She lifted the napkin, and the warm scent of venison flooded from under it. "Deer steak. Mister Beasley shot a doe and brought some over for you."

"Beasley, the hardware man?"

Nodding, she set the tray in his lap.

"What's he want to bring me food for?"

"He likes you."

"He don't even know me."

"People know you better than you think," she said. "Sometimes from the minute they meet you."

He looked at her in question, but she turned away. Walking over to the window, she looked out, much the same way Cully'd done. Almost as if, like the cowboy, she had some reason for not wanting to face him.

The light of the setting sun was golden. It glowed in her hair and framed her body as she reached up to draw the blind.

He watched her, wondering about the thoughts she stirred in him. In the time he'd been here, with her tending him, paying so much attention to him, the vague feelings had been growing into definite notions. He asked himself uncertainly whether he had the right to have such thoughts about her.

And what were her feelings? How much of her concern was just a woman's tenderness? Was there anything more to it than that?

She pulled the blind part way, and the light in the room softened to a twilight dimness. As she came to the table to light the lamp, she asked, "Eben, what are you planning to do when you're well again?"

"Go back to the valley and prove out the homestead."

"But you can't!" She looked at him, her forehead creasing in a frown. The match she'd lit flickered, as if her hand trembled. "Next time, Starrett will kill you!"

He shook his head. "Nobody's managed to kill me yet. I don't think Starrett will."

"But Eben—!"

"No, ma'am. I can't quit this. I've *got* to beat him."

"You can't do it alone," she said, her voice pleading with him not to try. The flame of the match was reflected in her eyes. She stood holding it, the lamp forgotten.

"Look out, you'll burn your fingers."

For an instant, she didn't seem to know what he meant. Then she looked at the match. Lifting the chimney, she put it to the wick. It caught, brightening the room. In the stronger light, he saw that there were teardrops on her lashes.

"Did it burn you?" he asked.

She shook her head slightly. Drawing a sharp breath, she tried to blink the tears away. One broke loose and slid down her cheek. She turned quickly, as if she didn't want him to see it.

He knew it wasn't burnt fingers that had caused the tears. Incredulous, he said, "You ain't crying for me?"

"No! Damn you, Eben Hawkins!" It was uncommon hard language for her to use. From the sobbing sound of her voice, she wasn't managing to hold back the tears.

He wanted to say something, to comfort her somehow. But he didn't know the way.

She jerked open the door. "No! I don't give a hoot about you, you stubborn, ornery, cantankerous mule!" she snapped as she dashed out, slamming it hard behind her.

He stared at it, knowing she didn't mean what she'd said. He wasn't at all sure just what she had meant. The notion he studied on was one he didn't quite dare to believe.

# CHAPTER 13

THE SUMMER WAS DRAGGING PAST IN A TEDIOUSLY slow way. Eagerness to get back to the farm gnawed at Eben. When he spoke of it, both Alice and Cully protested. But it was weakness rather than their words that had kept him from it this long.

His strength was steadily coming back, though. The first time he'd gotten out of bed, he'd barely been able to keep to his feet without Cully's support. For a long while, he'd had to have the cowboy's help when he tried to walk. Now he was strolling out alone, drifting around town, watching the cars roll past, and waiting for a time when the feeling of complete exhaustion didn't hit him so suddenly.

He'd begun to know people in Garrison. They were friendly folk who seemed really interested in what he'd done in the valley. Not just how he'd almost been killed but the farm work. People asked him a lot about it. They didn't ask about other things, like where he'd come from or what he'd done before he came to town. After a while, he'd got used to their questions. He'd even begun to get the hang of talking sociably with them. It was turning out to be easier than he'd expected.

The days in town weren't unpleasant. It was just that they were growing shorter and cooler. Impatience about the homestead chafed at him. He'd lost all the time he'd put into work as well as the time he'd been laid up healing. Close onto three months. Almost half of the time he had to get moved onto the land and busy improving it if he wanted to hold the homestead right he'd claimed.

At last the day came that he felt well enough to take care of himself beyond hollering distance of help. He didn't mention it to Alice or Cully. He just sneaked out his blanket, rifle, and a few supplies when neither one of them was around.

Mister Anchor, who ran the stable, looked him down doubtfully when he asked for the hire of a saddle horse.

"You *sure* you're up to riding?"

"Yeah, I'm fine." He knew he was still pale and gaunted, but the cramped pain in his chest had dwindled to a small dull ache that he'd got used to. His arm was out of the sling now, and even if his hand was almost useless, it hardly hurt at all. Except when he tried to flex it. He had it hidden in his pocket. Facing Anchor, he said with determination, "I know what I'm doing."

The stableman seemed doubtful. Sighing, he said, "All right. I'll give you Kelly. He's the best horse I got that handles easy and has some ginger. You take care with him, will you?"

"Sure," Eben answered, thinking he'd be damned careful. He couldn't afford to lose another horse to Starrett. Especially one he didn't own.

It was a bay geld with more the size and shape of an

eastern bred than one of the wild mountain ponies. It stood so peaceably to be mounted that he was afraid Anchor was trying to trick him out with a used-up nag. But it looked like a good horse, and when he lifted reins, it stepped out lively. In a short while, he decided the stableman had given him a really fine mount. It was a favor, and he appreciated it.

Riding into the woods was like coming awake after a long rest. The cool, brisk scent of the pines stirred the blood in him. He felt very alive. For the pleasure of it, he put the bay into a long lope.

He ran out of breath too quick, but it wasn't with a feeling of exhaustion. Easing the horse to an amble, he patted its withers and laughed. A chittering squirrel mocked him from a nearby branch.

Even at an easy gait, the tall horse covered ground quickly. It was still bright daylight when he reached the bluff overlooking the farm. Shifting in the saddle, he gazed out across the land.

There were heaps of char where his pole shack had been, but the valley'd begun to heal its scars. Wild grasses grew deep into the rubble of both cabins. The whole bottoms was a solid mat of long grass, just starting to change its brilliant summer green for autumn gold. It grew over the earth he'd turned with his plow. Tasseled stalks of corn mingled with it where he'd hoed and poked seed into the ground near the rocks.

Deer grazed out from the edges of the forest. A ways down, close to the creek, he could make out a red lump of an animal that he realized was the ox.

Grinning, he said softly, "Eat hearty, old cow. There's gonna be plenty of work for the two of us right soon."

How long until the first snow, he wondered. And how much could he hope to get done by then? He looked at the twisted hand, trying to flex it. The fingers wouldn't open or close all the way and they wouldn't work separate of each other.

The doctor'd told him that if he used the hand it would get stronger but that he couldn't expect very much improvement in it. Still, it was better than an iron hook, he supposed. He pressed the palm against the saddle horn. It took aching effort, but the fingers did close to grip.

He stepped down and unslung his rifle. Settling on the ground, he put the butt to his left shoulder. It felt all wrong. His left hand seemed awkward on the action. Bracing against his knee, he sighted carefully on a thick branch within easy range and squeezed the trigger.

It jerked bad, the gun wobbling in his hands. The shot was a far miss.

He tried it again and again until he'd emptied the magazine. Fumbling, he reloaded. There hadn't been one single hit. Not even a decently close miss. It would take a lot of practice to get the hang of shooting left-handed. Until then, the rifle wasn't going to be of much real use to him.

The sense of pleasure and vitality were gone. With a weary sigh, he owned to himself that it would be pure foolishness to try staying on the farm when he couldn't defend himself.

He stepped up onto the horse and looked back. There wasn't much hope of getting a cabin built he could live in before the snows came. No hope at all of any kind of a crop before spring.

As he lifted rein, he muttered a soft curse. If Jasper hadn't caught him, he'd have been living there now, eating from his own garden. Maybe he could even have made some cash by cutting of that wild grass for hay.

He sure could have hunted and trapped enough meat to keep himself fed through the winter.

Only Jasper had caught him, so he had a dull pain in his chest, a half-dead hand, and nothing but ashes for the hard work he'd done. Feeling tired and beaten, he turned the horse back toward Garrison.

He dreaded going back into the town. He didn't want to hole up in the walled rooms, behind the closed doors, with their stench of smoke and men. He didn't want to spend the winter futilely thinking and remembering.

Dammit—he couldn't let himself be beaten this easy—couldn't surrender the land to Starrett without at least one more try. Only what could he do?

Shifting the reins, he wrapped them onto his right hand and dug the left into his pocket. It was stuffed with the money Cully had brought him. Over forty dollars and he still had most of it.

Could a person reregister a homestead once that first six months had run out on him, he wondered, or did the government only give a man one chance?

The land agent in Cheyenne would know, he thought as he turned the horse eastward.

He rode on into darkness, then settled by starlight to eat and roll up in his blanket. It was a chill night. He woke to a cold dawn. But the sun rising in the east was a fire that should warm the day. Determined, he headed toward it.

It was late when he reached Cheyenne. He was afraid it might be too late for him to find the land office open. But as he dropped off his horse, he saw a glare of light behind the window. He could see McCracken putting a match to a lamp. That brought back mixed memories. But the last time he'd seen him, the agent had been friendly. He wondered if the man might remember him.

Striding across the walk, he rattled at the door.

McCracken set down the lamp and squinted toward the window. He was scowling as he came to the door.

Eben felt a dark discouragement. But as the door opened to him, he began, "I'm Eben Haw—"

"Hell, I know you." The scowl became a smile of welcome. "Come on in, Hawkins. Good to see you up and around."

"You know I'd been sick?" he asked in surprise, as he stepped into the office.

"Sure. Everyone knows. You've been the talk of Cheyenne City. You and your war with that rancher."

"The hell! How come?"

"News spreads in these parts. Set down. Have a drink." McCracken pulled a bottle out of a desk drawer. He dug up a glass and tilted the bottle over it. As he held it out, he added, "Pretty near came to a shooting over at the Palace a few weeks back. Couple of cowboys got to auguring your right to the land. They'd have shot each other about it, only the marshal got there in time."

As he perched himself on the edge of the desk, Eben asked suspiciously, "Was one a sandy-headed feller with a little scrawny moustache, blue eyes, and freckles, calls himself Cully?"

"That's him all right. He's the one who's been doing most of the talking about you. Seems to know it all."

"Damn him, he oughta know better'n that."

"He ain't done you any harm by it. Got half the town riled up against Starrett for you."

"I'd sooner he hadn't."

"Why not?"

"I got troubles enough already. Don't need folks nosing into my business."

"That ain't exactly the way of it." The agent settled

169

into the chair behind the desk and leaned back. He sipped from the bottle, then said, "Folks around here think right well of you. Lot of 'em be glad to help you out any way they can."

"Help?"

"I'll tell you how it is. Right now times aren't good, especially back in the States. Business slump seems to have been getting worse all summer. Ask me, I'd say it's building to a panic. Folks passing through town, looking for work, can't seem to find it anywhere. But *you* now—if you've come to Cheyenne looking for a job, you'll find one. There's folks here will be sure of it. They'll find it for you."

Eben gazed at him in amazement a moment before he answered, "I ain't looking for work. I'm looking to find out about my homestead. I ain't gonna have a cabin built again and more improvements by snowfall. Ain't gonna have nothing. What I want to know is will I be able to file again after that six months runs out on me."

"You're still figuring on holding that place?" McCracken was eying his twisted hand.

"Ain't I got the right?"

"Sure you have. only—"

"It's good land. I mean to keep it and to hell with Starrett." He flexed his fingers. It hurt. But there'd be more strength in them, in time. "You ought to see the grass growing there. If I'd been able, I could of took a crop of hay off this season. No planting or nothing. Just the wild grass. It's sure something to see."

"That's the grass Starrett's cattle feed off in the winter," the agent said.

Eben grinned slightly. "It'd sure set his gall to boiling if I was to mow out a good piece of it, huh?"

Nodding, McCracken grinned back at him.

170

He glanced through the window at the sharp clearness of the twilight sky. "How much time you s'pose is left 'fore the weather breaks bad?"

"You ain't thinking of really doing it?"

"I might could."

McCracken considered. "Don't know how it is in the valley, but it's been slow and dry over here. Might hold good a couple weeks more. Maybe as much as a month."

"I'd need get hold of a team and wagon. Have to clear out the old road into the place," Eben said in speculation. "Don't s'pose I could cut maybe a half acre a day by hand. Look at that grass, though, it'd give me nigh three ton to the acre. I might could cut and haul enough to pay hire on the wagon—*if* there's somebody in these parts who'd buy it."

"Army buys a lot of hay for the forts," the agent told him enthusiastically. "There's old Laramie and Fetterman up to the north and Russell and Sanders to the west and—"

"Hold on! Working alone, I'd be lucky to get—" He cut himself short and sighed. "Hell, I start trying to cut hay there, I'd get shot down 'fore I could rake a cock."

"Yeah," McCracken agreed sadly. "Whatever you do in that valley, you'd sure better not try it alone."

"Alone is what I am," Eben muttered, glancing at his hand. "Just me and a red ox, and can't neither one of us shoot worth a damn."

Leaning forward to fill his glass for him again, the agent said, "Well, it was a fine idea. I'd sure like to see Starrett's face if somebody was to cut so much as one acre of that grass."

He sipped at the whisky. It was smooth and warming. And a temptation. He wondered how much of it he'd need to wash away the feeling of weary discouragement. *Like water washing away rock,* his thoughts reminded him. He drew a deep breath and felt the small aching spot in his chest. Whisky wouldn't cure that.

He said, "I owe Starrett a debt."

"For what?"

"Piece of lead he had one of his hired hands give me."

McCracken eyed him with curiosity. "What you figure to do?"

"Cut grass! I'll cut as damned much of it as I can. If I can't haul it out and sell it, I'll rake it into the creek and let it rot!"

"Look, I got an idea. Feller up the road has a small sort of freight business. He's got wagons and he's always looking for a dollar. Likely he'd contract the hauling for you. Maybe take it on shares."

"I doubt I could cut enough by myself to interest him."

"Not just you alone. Hire yourself some men. Go in and mow as much grass as you can. As long as you intend to have Starrett bust a gut, give him a *good* reason. Make yourself a profit doing it."

"Hire men?"

The agent nodded vigorously. "Like I said, times are bad back East right now. Plenty of men drifting through looking for nigh any kind of work. Men who'll hire on cheap. Some would likely work just for found, the way things are."

"Sure," Eben grunted. It was a fine handsome idea. But even if he could make a deal for haulage and if he could find the men and could afford to pay them and feed them, how long would they be able to work before Starrett and his bunch attacked? How many men would hire on if they knew they were going to be attacked?

172

He asked, "What about my claim on the land? Can I file a second time?"

"Far as I'm concerned, you won't need to," the agent told him. "You've been making improvements. If you got hit with a storm or struck by lightning, the land office wouldn't hold it against you. Way I figure, Starrett's just as much a natural disaster as those would be."

"I'm obliged," he said, shrugging to settle the rifle slung on his shoulder. "Real obliged."

As he opened the door to leave, McCracken called after him, "You think on what I suggested."

He thought on it. He drifted along the street, glancing casually into shop windows and thinking it was a hell of a fine idea—just impossible. He couldn't hope for anyone else to take a hand in *his* troubles.

His only chance would be to get to work in the valley alone and hope that Starrett wouldn't discover him before he'd done some real damage, as far as the grass went. Even that was a slim chance. A damn fool thing to consider when he knew he couldn't handle the rifle.

Probably end up on a rope again, dragged till he was dead, the way Jake had been, he told himself.

A window caught his attention. Stopping, he gazed thoughtfully at the double-barreled shotgun. The placard said it was a central-fired ten-bore gun made by E. M. Reilly and Company of London. He'd heard of them. It was a very handsome weapon.

A shotgun might could be damned handy, he thought. It lacked for the range of a rifle, but right now the Henry sure wouldn't be of much use to him at any range. With a shotgun he could at least keep anyone from getting close enough to put a rope on him again.

Studying on the idea, he walked into the store.

173

The shopkeeper was anxious to make a sale, but he wouldn't take less than cash for the Reilly gun. And the price was right high.

After some talk, he showed Eben another twin-barrel he'd be willing to trade for the Henry, the pocket pistol, and a little boot.

"It ain't exactly a Greener," he said as he opened the breech for Eben to have a look. "But it's England-made on about the same plan. It'll give you just as good service."

Eben examined it thoroughly as they discussed it. He was satisfied with the look of it. The shopkeeper warranted it to be sound and accurate. Eventually, they struck a bargain.

With the brown-paper-wrapped shotgun in his good hand and his pocket stuffed full of buck-loaded shells, he stepped out onto the walk again.

The sun was gone. The dark sky was flecked with a mass of stars. Lamps along the street spilled bright puddles of light onto the walk. Sounds of talking, of laughter, and of fiddle music tumbled through an open door not far ahead. The scents of beer and whisky mingled with odors of men and coal-oil smoke.

On impulse, he went in. For a long while, he stood at the bar sipping a whisky and thinking about the valley.

To his surprise, he realized that he was enjoying being in the saloon, surrounded by the music and the voices.

A man might really find pleasure in coming into town and being among other folk, he thought. It was a strange new idea. As he studied on it, he recalled someone saying as how other settlers would follow him if he managed to hold on in the valley. He'd dreaded that thought back then. But now it came to him that it might not be so bad after all. Hell, there might even be some good in having a few neighbors, once he got settled.

He looked at his reflection in the backbar mirror, wondering if he ever would get settled. The odds were sure running strong against it.

But he didn't want to think about odds or the possibility of losing. The thing a man needed was determination. Like water on rock, he just had to keep at it steady. Not let anything sway him or scare him off. He'd win eventually.

He finished his drink and picked up the shotgun to leave. The wrapping paper was coming loose. He fumbled at it, silently cursing the near-useless hand, then gave up and jerked the paper off. Tossing it away, he headed out onto the street.

He'd walked about half a block when the shout brought him up sharp.

*"Hawkins!"*

The voice was whisky-slurred but fierce and wild. He recognized it.

A feeling like ice prickled at the back of his neck and tightened his throat as he wheeled. He saw Jasper standing on the walk in a circle of lamplight. It reflected on the brass-bound revolver that was aimed toward Eben.

"G'damn you, Hawkins!" Jasper hollered. "This time I kill you, you'll *stay* dead!"

Eben could feel the dull ache in his chest and remember the sound of bone grating on bone. He gazed coldly at Jasper.

There were images of the lamp's flame in the man's glistening eyes. Sweat shone on his hard-set face and dampened his untrimmed beard. He burned inside with his own anger. He burned with a want—a *need*—to kill.

The people on the walk around Eben knew it, too. He was aware of them darting away from him, leaving the space around him clear. He stood alone.

Grinning, Jasper savored the moment of anticipation. He licked at his lips. His eyes probed Eben, hunting for fear.

There wasn't a damned thing to lose, Eben thought wearily. Thumbing back one hammer, he swung up the shotgun. He caught the barrel across his bad hand, leveling it at Jasper's gut.

In the harsh silence, the cock of the second hammer was as sharp as the crack of lightning.

Jasper'd been too intent on his own plans and thoughts. He hadn't noticed the shotgun before. That much was obvious. He'd been hunting fear. He found the blank dark bores of the twin barrels. They were suddenly staring at him.

He stared back. The muscles of his face went rigid. Shadows grooved deep into his skin. Sweat gleamed on it like oil. His hand tightened convulsively on the revolver.

Eben took a step toward him.

His gaze held locked to the muzzles of the shotgun. He couldn't pull free from them. Frantically, he jerked at the pistol, triggering it. The wild shot spanged into the plank wall at Eben's side.

Another step.

Despite the warm tones of the lamplight, Jasper's face had a grayness to it. His lips quivered, shaping a word. But no sound came from them.

Trembling, he fired again.

Eben felt lead snatch at his sleeve, stinging his arm. He needed one more step. He took it.

A sickly white rimmed Jasper's eyes as he gazed at

the shotgun. He shuddered with sudden violence. Fighting the shivering of his hand, he hauled back the pistol's hammer. It was aimed toward Eben's chest. Too close now to miss.

Eben heard the scear catch. He jumped. Twisting to the side, away from the pistol, he swung the shotgun up over his shoulder.

Butt first, he rammed it toward Jasper's face.

Something snapped. He felt the jar in his wrists. For an instant, he thought he'd cracked the stock.

The pistol slammed its roar against his ears. Bitter smoke burned his eyes. But the shot went wild.

Blinking, he saw Jasper fall back and spill to the ground, limp as grain poured from a sack. He had the shotgun up, ready to club it at the man again. But there was no need of it.

Jasper lay with arms and legs outflung awkwardly. His head twisted to an impossible angle. His eyes were open, staring in horror, as if they still saw the muzzles of the shotgun.

The silence became a hum of muttering. A man came forward. Dropping to his knees at Jasper's side, he touched the gray face, then looked toward Eben.

"Deader'n a rail spike. Neck's busted."

Eben nodded.

Someone else said thinly, "I never seen the like of it before."

"What the hell's going on here?"

Eben knew that voice too well. It was the town marshal's. He wheeled to face the lawman who pushed through the crowd that had suddenly surrounded him.

"Little difference of opinion," the man kneeling by the body said. His face was like old leather, scruffed with a streaked gray beard. It crinkled as he grinned.

"Slight fallin' out."

"Hell on wheels again," someone added.

The marshal's eyes narrowed on Eben. His voice was hard, cold as a steel blade. "Hawkins! Knew you were trouble on the hoof. Knew it the first minute I ever seen you."

"No!" Eben snapped. He held the shotgun in both hands, gripping it tight. He didn't notice the pain surging up his right arm. "No, dammit! You ain't jailing me this time!"

"No?" the marshal growled.

Eben shook his head. "Not for something that ain't my fault."

"It looks to me like you've just killed a man."

"*He* begun it. He shot at me more'n once 'fore I clubbed him."

"That's right," the graybeard volunteered. He prodded a finger at the body. "This'un started shooting. Got off three, four shots 'fore this young feller laid him out."

Still eying Eben, the marshal said suspiciously, "Three or four shots and they all missed?"

The graybeard answered before Eben could. "Yes, sir! Young feller pointed that shotgun at him. Got him too shaking scared to hit anything. Just walked up and whomped him with the butt of it."

"Yeah!" a cowboy in the crowd said breathlessly. Stepping forward, he called to Eben, "How come, mister? How come you hit him that way? Why didn't you just shoot him down?"

"The gun ain't loaded."

"Huh?" the graybeard grunted in astonishment. He stared at the gun in Eben's hands, then began to chuckle. "Damn! That's the double-barrel damndest

178

thing I ever seen."

"You expect me to believe all that?" the lawman said, Eben nodded. "It's the truth."

"You better come on to my office with me."

"Not under arrest, I won't!" He lifted the shotgun slightly, as if he meant to heft it as a club again.

"Don't threaten me. I represent the law around here."

"I ain't broke your damned law. I've *never* broke your damned law around here. I ain't being jailed again for something that ain't my fault!"

The bystanders crowded in closer, buzzing among themselves. One of them spoke up. "He's right, marshal. He was only defending himself."

Scowling, the lawman turned to look at them. Others muttered in tones of agreement. He picked out men, calling them by name, and asked if they'd seen it happen. Most admitted they had.

"I'll need statements from witnesses," he told them. He faced Eben again. "You're coming with me. Hold on! You're not under arrest. Not yet. I've got to get the straight of this business. In my office."

Gazing at him coldly, Eben considered. It had to be settled. With a nod, he said, "All right."

The marshal sighed. Gesturing for the men he'd called to follow, he started toward his office. Eben strode along at his side, still gripping the shotgun hard enough for it to hurt.

# CHAPTER 14

WHEN HE'D FINISHED SPEAKING HIS PIECE, EBEN WAS left to wait in the back room while the marshal talked to

179

the witnesses. Eben sat with his chin cupped in his good hand and the smell of the jail stirring a nausea in his belly. The stubble on his jaw itched.

He'd gotten no answer and no sign of a decision from the marshal.

It hadn't been his fault. He told himself they couldn't hold him and try him for it. This was nothing like the time before, when *he* had been the one who attacked. That time, he'd thought he had damned good reason to kill. But it had taken over seven years before someone came around to his way of thinking and the governor had pardoned him of it.

If he was asked, he couldn't deny that he'd done a killing before. It might go hard against him if they tried him now. And a man couldn't much wait seven years on the end of a rope while somebody decided maybe he'd had good reason after all.

It took time for the marshal to hear out each of the witnesses. But at last it was done. With a weary sigh, he told Eben that he was free to go.

The sense of relief was dull. Eben felt hollow and brittle, too exhausted to square away his own thoughts. He stepped out of the office, expecting it to be near dawn. But the wait hadn't been as long as it had felt. The street lamps were still lit, the saloons open, and people milled on the walks.

Several men were hanging around the office door as he came out. They looked like they were waiting. He pushed hurriedly past them.

"Mister!" one called at him. "Hey, mister, you're Hawkins, ain't you?"

He gave no sign of hearing but kept on walking. He hoped he could get away from them. He didn't want company now. He damned well didn't want to talk

180

about Jasper's death.

The man grabbed at his arm.

Twisting, he jerked free and glared at the stranger. "Leave me be!"

"Please, Mister Hawkins, I got to talk to you. I'm Mike Healy and I'm a good worker."

It made no sense to Eben. Ignoring the man, he turned away. But the hand clutched at him again.

"I heard you're hiring farm hands, Mister Hawkins," Healy pleaded. "I'm good at it. Had my own place once. Please! I *got* to find work."

Another man pushed up to his side. "Me, too!"

"I'm not the one you're looking for," Eben said.

"You're Eben Hawkins, ain't you? From Clear Creek Valley?" Healy asked, his expression painful with the fear that he was wrong.

Eben understood. It had to have been McCracken talking about that notion to mow hay in the valley. Silently he cursed himself for having trusted someone else with his plan. Now word would get to Starrett. There'd be no time at all to cut grass before the rancher interfered.

A third man had been watching. He stepped forward and asked, "You still aiming to work your homestead in that valley, Hawkins?"

"What concern is it of yours?"

"I'm a farmer myself. Tried to take land there a year ago. Let that damned cowman spook me out, and it's been galling me ever since. You figure you can lick him?"

Eben nodded.

"I'll tell you something," the farmer said. "A feller lets himself get run off the way I did, it gets to where he's 'shamed to look in a mirror. Since I started hearing how you'd held on up there, I'm sick of the sight of myself. If you need help on your place, you got it!"

"Starrett ain't backed down any threats," Eben told him. "He's had a good try at killing me already, and he'll try it again. Anybody else goes into that valley for farming, he'll do as much for them.'"

"To hell with Starrett! I had a nice piece of land picked for myself up there. I mean to have it back. It'll be that much harder for Starrett if there's a couple of us, won't it? If you need help, you got it."

"Hey, look!" Healy interrupted. "Mister Hawkins, I asked you first. If you're hiring, I *need* the work. I'm hungry."

"Working for me could get you killed," Eben said.

"I could die of starving, too. You need somebody as will fight, all right. Hell, I've fought the English in Ireland, the rats in the bilge coming over, and the Rebs in the States when I got here. If fighting's the only kind of work I can get, I'll take it."

"Me, too," the second man put in.

"Who are you?" Eben asked him.

"Leach. I never fought the English, but I was in the war. I'll fight," he said hopefully.

Eben looked the two of them over as he considered. Healy was big and broad through the shoulders, with dark, curly hair and a face that should have been round and full. But it was gaunted, stained with coal smoke. He had the look of a hungry man.

So did Leach. He was smaller, light-boned with a thin, pinched face. He looked as if he'd been hungry all his life.

They were both in worn clothing that was beginning to tatter. Both had been traveling, searching. He could sense their desperation. They brought back vivid memories of Andersonville.

Thoughtfully, he said, "I ain't been planning on hiring nobody. And I ain't got much money."

"I don't need much," Leach answered. "I'd work for a decent meal."

Healy nodded in agreement.

Several of them could sure cut a lot more grass than one man with a crippled up hand, Eben told himself. Maybe enough to make a load or two for sale. But there wasn't a damned chance of doing it in secret now. They'd have to have a way of holding off Starrett while they worked. Three or four men wouldn't make awork crew and a line of defense as well.

But another thought was shaping itself for him. Thrusting his good hand into the pocket with the money in it, he said, "S'pose I could offer you five dollars each for the fighting, and shares if we could make any money at the working?"

"Mister, I'd jump at it," Healy answered.

"Me, too!" Leach put in.

Eben turned to the farmer. "You *sure* you want in on this trouble, Mister—?"

"Name's Salem and I'm faunching for it."

"Can you get hold of a wagon and team?"

"I got 'em. Studebaker wagon and a fine span of Arkansas rabbits. Got 'em with me. Druv 'em into town."

"You know you could lose 'em to Starrett?" he offered in warning.

Salem nodded. "I'd sooner lose my wagon than my pride."

"All right. S'pose you take this, Mister Salem." He pulled a greenback out of his pocket. "You and these fellers see if you can stir up somebody as will sell you a couple of hay scythes. Supplies, too. Flour and such, maybe a sack of beans, and some side meat. That suit you fellers?"

"Damn well!" Healy said. Leach nodded vigorously.

"And a can of coal oil," Eben added. "Take what's left of the money to get a decent store-bought meal. Then meet me out on the road west of town. 'fore you leave, spread the word around that you're going up to Clear Creek Valley to cut hay."

"Spread the word?" Salem repeated in question.

"I want to be sure Starrett gets wind of it," Eben said. "And if you should run on to a couple more fellers willing to do some fighting, same as us, I'd be real glad to have 'em along."

"I know some others as are hungry," Healy muttered.

Salem grinned. "Know a few who might be interested, myself."

"I mean it when I say *fighting,*" Eben warned. "This could turn into outright war."

"Yes sir!" Healy snapped him a mock salute. "An army travels on its belly, sir."

"You better go get yourselves fed, then."

He watched them head up the street. It was a hell of a strange feeling to have men working with him—looking to him to lead them. Getting himself killed was one thing. Leading other men off to a fight was something different. Something awesome.

Frowning, he studied on it as he started after his horse.

There wasn't much of a moon. When he passed the edge of town, he realized just how dim the light was. Riding slowly, he let his eyes adjust. He decided it was bright enough for them to travel the well-worn wheel ruts outside of Cheyenne. Once they got to the woods

184

where they'd need light, the sun would be up.

Halting on the empty road, he turned the horse. He leaned an arm on the saddle horn and gazed at the glow of the town lights, wondering if the men would come. Mightn't they change their minds once they'd thought it over?

He'd got his plan pretty well worked out, either way. By himself, he could harass hell out of Starrett. But the bunch of them might be able to force the rancher to bargain—this time to *his* terms. Alone, he could keep fighting. With help, he might be able to win. He hoped desperately that the men would come.

He heard the wagon before he saw it. The mules were in a fast trot. Salem hauled on the reins, grinning broad enough for it to show in the dull light.

As Eben heeled the horse up alongside, the farmer said happily, "We brung along a couple of friends."

Eben looked at the shadowed figures crouching in the back of the wagon. He frowned uncertainly as he counted eight of them.

"Look, I ain't got a lot of money. Maybe enough to pay four, five men. Not everybody."

"There's some of us plan to take our pay in land, Mister Hawkins," one of them answered, holding up a rifle. "If we break Starrett's hold on that valley, some of us plan to homestead there."

"I'd do it myself if I could raise a stake," Healy muttered. "I'd sure like to own land again."

"Maybe you can. Working together, maybe we all can," Eben said huskily. There was a taut elation building in him. An eagerness.

He edged the horse closer and swung off it into the wagon. Putting down the shotgun, he looped the horse's reins loosely on the tailgate chain.

"S'pose we get moving," he said as he settled himself. "I can tell you what I got in mind while we're covering ground. We got to get there well ahead of Starrett. Got some setting up to do."

"You're sure he'll come?" one of the men asked.

"Yeah." He was grinning to himself. Starrett might just send a sharpshooter or a couple of hired hands to finish off a lone man. But he wouldn't pull anything like that on a bunch of them. No, he'd ride in at the head of his troops with a grand show of force and try to scare hell out of them first. Only he'd be in for a mite *of* a surprise.

They'd covered a good distance before they stopped to camp out what was left of the night. In the morning they got an early start. With the gang of them and the span of mules, it didn't take long to clear the old wagon road into the valley. By twilight, they had it open. But they stayed to the woods to make their camp that night. And Eben posted pickets.

At dawn they headed into the open. The four men who split off to go up onto the slopes would be fairly safe. If things went wrong, they'd be able to retreat. Eben and the five who stayed with him in the field were the ones who'd be facing Starrett.

A man named Vanders took the first watch from the ledge on the scarp, while Eben and the others made a show with the cutting of grass along the spring stream.

The morning went peacefully, and that was bad. Waiting for trouble stretched a man's nerves out worse than facing it. Tension, as much as working under the bright sun, soaked Eben's shirt and slicked his palms with sweat. His injured hand ached with the effort of holding a grip on the scythe. He couldn't keep pace with

186

the others, and he cursed himself for it.

The sun was into the west when he completed his own turn at watch and came down the scarp again. He wondered how the hell long it would take Starrett to show. Maybe not today at all. Maybe not even tomorrow. That idea frightened him. His nerves were taut-drawn. He wasn't sure he could take many days of this kind of waiting without snapping.

Peeling his shirt, he knelt by the stream and scooped cold water into his face. He flinched as a flung rock splashed into the water. Swallowing, he looked over his shoulder in question.

The man on the ledge was waving and gesturing excitedly toward the ranch road. When Eben acknowledged the signal, he ducked back out of sight.

Eben called softly to the men in the field. They dropped their tools, picked up weapons and headed for cover. Healy and Leach crawled under the wagon with borrowed revolvers in their hands. Salem and Vanders, with rifles, took to the rocks. Heading in the other direction, Edwards dropped to his belly behind a heap of charred logs and readied his single-shot sporting rifle. Eben went to the wagon.

He stood with the cocked shotgun in both hands, listening intently. As he caught faint sounds from the forest, he stepped back between the wagon and the scarp.

The sounds grew louder. It was another trick of some kind, he thought. The riders were making too much noise, and it sounded like there weren't more than a couple of them.

Dammit, he wanted Starrett to show openly. He wanted to begin with face-to-face talk, not shooting.

The voice that hollered his name from the woods

startled him. He shouted back, "Cully?"

Calling in reply, the cowboy plunged his horse into the open. Eben winced at the sight of the rider following close behind him. It was Alice.

He strode from the wagon to meet them, glaring at Cully. "What the devil are you doing out here!"

With an embarrassed grin, Cully reined in his horse "Heard you'd come up to cut grass. Rode out to watch."

"The hell! Dammit, don't you understand what we're doing?"

Alice was having trouble with her horse. She perched awkwardly on the sidesaddle. One hand clutched the horse's mane. As she tugged the reins with the other, the horse tossed its head, snorting.

Eben caught the bridle with his good hand. Pulling the animal steady, he looked up at her. "You got no business out here! Not now!"

She slid down and grabbed at his arms. "Eben!" The one word was a sigh of relief, of fear and worry, of hope and pleading. She gazed into his face.

"You got no business here," he repeated. He turned toward Cully. "Dammit, you hadn't no business bringing her out!"

"Hell, Hawk, I couldn't leave you start a fight without I was along to join in. And she wouldn't let me come up without her." Suddenly the grin faded. Deeply serious, the cowboy said, "She *had* to see you again, Hawk."

"You're looking for trouble here, aren't you?" she said, clinging to Eben's arms. Her fingers dug deep into his flesh. "You *want* Starrett to attack you."

"I'm trying to put an end to the trouble, once and for all," he answered. "Now, you get on that horse. Get back to Garrison. Ride all night if you have to, but don't stop until you're back home."

"No!"

*"Yes!"* He scooped her up in his arms, hefting her toward the saddle. But the horse shied back from her sudden flailing. And Eben staggered with the cumbersome bulk of her. She wasn't heavy, but she struggled wildly, and he hadn't his full strength. He couldn't manage it. Angry with himself, he let her down.

She grabbed his wrist, protesting. "Don't, Eben, please! He'll kill you! Let him have the land!"

"I'd got to finish this," he said. "It ain't just for me. It's for you, too."

"No, no, no! I don't want the land. I don't care about it. I want *you!*"

It was the answer to a question he hadn't dared ask. He stood looking into her eyes, listening to his own wild thoughts.

He had to keep to the matter at hand. Slowly and quietly, he said, "I *can't* quit. This business is more than ever I knew it was going to be. It's something that was started before I come here. I've took myself a part in it, and now I got to keep at it till it's finished. You have to understand that."

She searched his face. Hesitantly, she nodded. "Then I'm staying with you."

"No, ma'am. You're going back to Garrison."

"I won't! I can't let you fight Starrett alone."

"I ain't alone." He glanced back. The men had come out of their holes. They stood watching silently. He gestured toward them. "There's a bunch of us together in this. We'll stand together against Starrett, and we'll beat him. Maybe we won't even have to fight It might be we can handle it all peaceable."

"Ain't likely," Cully grunted.

"Eben, please—" she said. "I know it's what you have to do. Please understand what I have to do. I've got to stay here with you."

He drew a deep breath as he groped for a way to answer her. "You wouldn't be helping me none' by it. You might hurt me if you stayed."

"How?"

"I got to have my mind on what I'm doing when Starrett shows up. I won't if you're here. I'll be bad worried if I don't know you're safe at home."

For a long moment, she gazed at him. At last she said, "Help me onto my horse, Eben."

As he took her hand, he looked toward Cully. "See she gets home all right, will you?"

"Hell, I come out here to fight!"

"Not with *me!* Please don't you give me trouble now."

The cowboy sighed and grumbled something deep in his throat. Gruffly, he said, "Soon as she's home, I'll be heading back."

"If Starrett shows, I'll ask him to wait for you," Eben muttered.

He helped Alice up onto her mount. She clung to his hand as she settled on the saddle. Her eyes shone moist. A tear rolled slowly down her cheek. Brushing at it with the back of her wrist, she said, "Promise me you'll come back?"

"I'm planning to."

"If you say you will, I *know* you will." She turned her mouth in a smile. It took effort. Tugging clumsily at the reins, she turned the horse away from him.

Cully kicked up his pony, taking the lead back toward the ranch road.

With a sense of relief that had him feeling drained of

strength, Eben watched them go. The hand he raised to wipe at his forehead was trembling.

Healy was grinning as he walked up, but his voice was serious. "So *that's* your reason?"

Eben nodded.

"Wish I had me a reason like that," Healy said.

Embarrassed, Eben muttered, "She's my brother's widow."

"Ain't nothing wrong with that. Not after a decent mournin' time's passed."

"No, I guess there ain't," he owned, picking up the scythe. He was grinning to himself as he set in to work again.

Grass fell before the blades. The shadows stretched out from the western ridges. Winds began to spill down the slopes, rustling through the woods. They stirred the trees, crackling branches and whispering among them.

Pausing, Eben scanned the forest. Maybe Starrett would attack after dark. Or maybe there'd be a long night of waiting, alert for danger, and another day of being bait.

He flexed his shoulders, stretching weary muscles. Suddenly he frowned and gazed toward the trees. Something had moved in the darkness under them. Maybe an animal. Maybe something else.

The man on watch hadn't given any signal. Eben glanced toward the ledge. He couldn't see the guard. He hoped to hell the man hadn't fallen asleep up there. A chilly apprehension lay along his spine.

The faint noise he heard sounded like a horse's nicker.

Picking up the shotgun, he called out softly to the men. He gestured for them to follow as he headed for the wagon.

191

He hadn't quite reached it when the riders appeared.

They came quietly from the forest, strung out along its edge. At first glance, he thought there must be thirty or more of them. But then he realized there weren't half that many.

They drew out of the woods in a line abreast, like cavalry preparing to charge. Some had rifles, and all seemed to have side arms. But the rifles rested across their saddle bows, and the handguns were holstered.

Starrett was at the center of the line, holding a taut rein on the big wild-eyed horse he straddled. With a signal to his men, he let it forward another stride. The two riders flanking him moved with him, but the rest held their positions.

With a sense of relief, Eben swallowed at the lump in his throat. The rancher meant to talk first.

It was a big horse for such a small man. Starrett sat it with his shoulders back and his spine ramrod stiff. Chin out defiantly, he glared at the men bunched by the wagon. "Is one of you Hawkins?"

Eben realized that this man who'd ordered his murder had never even seen his face. Holding the shotgun down in both hands, but cocked, he stepped forward. "I am."

"I want to talk to you," Starrett snarled. Under narrowed lids, his eyes were hot and angry.

Eben could almost feel the fire in that gaze. In a voice a damnsight calmer than he felt, he called back, "Come on over and talk."

Starrett walked the horse slowly forward. The flank riders stuck close at his sides. They were both taller men than their boss, but the big horse brought his head level with theirs.

Watching them, Eben knew that the rancher would tower over him from the saddle. He understood the advantage that would give Starrett. It was hard to stand firm bargaining with a man when you had to crane your neck back, as if you were down on your knees, just to look him in the face.

Moving casually, he stepped up onto a charred beam. It would make him as easy a target as a tin can on a fence rail. But it would put him a lot closer to level with Starrett. That was important. And maybe he wouldn't be a target. Maybe.

As Starrett drew rein, Eben glanced at the flank riders. He didn't recall having seen the one on the right before, but the one at the left was Pete. Meeting the rider's eyes, he nodded as if in greeting. Pete turned away. He gazed past Eben, at the rocks, looking damned uncomfortable.

"What the hell do you think you're doing here?" Starrett demanded.

"Cutting hay," Eben said.

"Not *my* hay! Not on *my* land, you ain't!"

"This ain't your land."

"This is my winter range. The whole valley. It's *mine*."

"No." He gave a slow shake of his head. "I got a right here. A lawful right. The government says this valley belongs to us people who are willing to live on it and work it. We mean to take it."

"I'll give you a piece of it," Starrett snapped at him. "You get the hell off it within ten minutes, or I'll give you six foot of it forever."

"No," he said again. "I got a hundred sixty acres here, most of it in grass . . ."

"You cut one more blade of my grass," Starrett interrupted, swinging his gaze to include the men by the wagon. "Any manjack of you touches one more blade of my grass, and he dies on the spot."

"This is *our* valley. If we don't cut this grass, there won't anybody get the use of it. Either we cut it, or we burn it."

"*What!*"

"We cut it, or we burn it," Eben repeated.

The anger in Starrett's eyes flared. Hot color flushed his face. "Of all the goddamn—you don't dare—you can't bluff me out, Hawkins! You raise a hand to touch this grass, and my men start shooting!"

"Let one of your men fire a shot," Eben said, holding his voice steady and quiet. He looked at Pete. "Fire one shot. *Not* at me, though."

The cowboy glanced to his boss for orders. He got a curt nod. Frowning in puzzlement, he pulled the revolver out of his holster. He pointed it toward the ground and triggered it.

The sharp blast echoed down the valley. Gesturing toward the slopes, Eben said, "Look yonder."

Starrett squinted as he scanned the ridges. Suddenly he winced. A faint puff of black smoke had appeared—smoke from oily rags and twisted torches of grass just fired. It rose in a thin wisp. Another curl of smoke drifted up from a different point along the slope. Then another. And another. They made ugly blurs against the sky before the wind wiped them away.

"It's a goddamned bluff," Starrett said. But his voice wasn't as strong and certain as it had been. "That ain't the graze burning."

"No, not yet. But if you won't let *us* have the grass, why should we leave it for *you* to use?"

"I'll kill you."

"Maybe you'll kill us standing here in front of you," Eben answered, "but what about them up there? One more shot's the signal they're waiting for. They hear it, they'll put those torches to the grass."

"Four, five men—four, five little fires. I can wipe you out and snuff that much fire before it does any damage."

"Maybe. *If* there's only four or five men up there. But are you *sure* of that?"

"You're trying to bluff me," Starrett snarled at him.

"Are you *sure?* How do you know there ain't more men you can't see from here. It might be every man you've kept out of this valley is on your range right now, ready to light a fire. How many men have you kept out of here, Starrett? How many cowboys you got guarding your beeves and your houses and barns right now? Grass is fair dry and there's a good wind. How many fires you s'pose it'd take to burn every blade of graze off every inch of land in these hills?"

The rancher's mouth moved, but the words caught in his throat, rumbling there like trapped thunder. His face twisted into hard ridges, dark as a storm about to break. Anger screamed in his eyes.

Fearfully, in a hushed, coaxing voice, Pete said, "Boss, maybe we ought—we got plenty of other places for winter graze—maybe—"

Starrett didn't seem to hear him. The fierce raging eyes were locked onto Eben. There was no yielding in them. And no reasoning. Nothing but hatred.

*It wasn't going to work:* The thought seared through Eben's mind. They'd tried and they'd lost. There was nothing left but to stand and die and hope to hell it wasn't all a waste.

Words broke through Starrett's taut throat, sharp-edged as steel.

"*Nobody* bucks *me*, Hawkins! I'll see you in hell!"

His hand clawed for the revolver on his thigh.

The shotgun hung cocked in Eben's hands. With a jerk of his right arm, he swung the muzzle up. The barrel quivered against his bad hand as he pulled a trigger.

It bucked hard, almost throwing itself out of his grip. It spat bright flame and spewed white smoke in the dusky twilight.

Through the stinging smoke, Eben saw Starrett flung back out of the saddle. The horse reared, snorting in panic and pain, as buckshot skimmed its neck. It rose, pawing frantically, and came down into a lurching, terrified gallop. The tattered, blood-smeared thing hung from one stirrup bounced at every stride, trailing dark stains and torn bits of itself in the grass.

Fighting the nausea that writhed in his belly, Eben swung the shotgun toward Pete. One hammer was still cocked.

The cowboy's horse twisted under him, straining at the bit. He struggled one-handed with it. His right arm hung at his side, the sleeve splotched red. The buckshot had spread.

Hauling at the reins, he glanced toward the runaway horse and hollered, "For Gawd's sake, somebody catch it!"

The other flank rider's eyes turned to Eben in question. There was an awed respect for the shotgun in them.

Eben nodded assent, and the man gigged his horse to race after the runaway. The line of men along the woods stood in place watching, waiting uncertainly. A murmur of shocked whispering ran among them.

They were like soldiers, Eben thought. They obeyed orders, and that was the whole of it.

Pete got his horse calmed. He clamped his hand to the

injured arm. His mouth was hard-set, grim with pain. There was fear in his eyes as he looked at the shotgun leveled at him. But there was defiance in his voice. "I reckon you mean that other barrel for me?"

Eben shook his head. "It ain't exactly you we've been fighting. It's Starrett. Only he's lost his war. If you're of a mind, I'd be damn glad to talk peace."

For a moment, Pete frowned in bewilderment. Then, slowly, understanding spread across his face. He looked back at the men. The murmuring stopped. They gazed at him.

One broke the silence. "He killed the boss . . ."

"You reckon he didn't have reason?" Pete snapped. "Gawddammit, I'm sick of this business! I'm sick of all of it. I don't *like* killing. Or dying!"

Turning to Eben again, he said, "You name your terms, mister."

"Go back home and leave us be," Eben answered. "That's all."

The man in the line grumbled sarcastically, "You gonna leave us keep our mounts and side arms?"

"Sure, Reb," Eben called back at him. "If you keep 'em out of this valley. Else you won't get the chance to take 'em out again."

As the man started to reply, Pete shouted at him, "You shut up! He *means* it!"

He looked to the riders at either side of him. No one spoke up in his behalf. Shoulders slumping, he made no answer.

"I don't want any more fighting," Eben said. "All I want here is to get this hay cut and get my cabin built. Put in a crop come spring. Make a home here. Most of these men with me, that's what they want, too."

The flank rider had caught the runaway and slung its

197

burden over the saddle. He was riding back toward them, leading the horse.

The feeling of sickness stirred in Eben's gut again as he glanced at it. Wearily, he added, "Just leave us be."

"I'd be glad to," Pete said sincerely. "Damn glad to. I ain't proud of what we've been doing. I swear you that, Hawkins."

Lifting rein, he started to turn away. He stopped sharp, scanning the slopes. Eben followed his gaze. Thin lines of orange cut through the sunset shadows. The signal shot had been fired. The grass was burning.

Pete wheeled toward the line of riders. "You fellers get the hell up there, put them damn fires out!" he snapped. Then, remembering, he looked back over his shoulder. "That all right with you, Hawkins?"

"I'd be obliged."

The cowboys hesitated.

"Dammit," Pete hollered. "Anybody who don't agree with me can stay here and augur *him!*" He nodded toward Eben. "The rest of you get up there and put out them fires!"

One man gigged his horse. The others began to follow until they were all strung out across the valley.

Eben turned to his own men. "Healy, go with 'em. Take my horse. Make sure the fighting's done."

Watching them, he told himself it was finished. He'd won. There was nothing left to do now but clean up the damage and start back to work.

Wearily, he stepped off the beam and sat down on it. As he started to sink his chin into his hand, he saw Pete riding toward the trail, his injured arm hanging at his side.

Clean up the damage, he repeated to himself. He called out, "Hey! Hey, Pete, you want to try patching up that arm 'fore you leave?"

The cowboy hesitated, looking back in question.

And Salem came up to Eben's side to ask, "What the hell you mean to do? You want to help one of *them*?"

"This war is over, ain't it? They're helping us put out the fires we started, ain't they?" He watched Pete slowly turn the horse and head back toward him. "Hell, if we're gonna settle here, it won't hurt us none to be friendly with our neighbors. *All* our neighbors."

"I reckon so," Salem muttered thoughtfully.

There was a star glimmering against the violet sky. Eben gazed at it. "I s'pose I'd better go into Cheyenne tomorrow. Face the law about what's happened here."

"You won't have no trouble over it," Salem assured him. "Everybody seen he meant to kill you. You *had* to shoot him."

"Yeah," he sighed. A man did what he had to.

"Maybe you ought to go by way of Garrison," Salem was saying. "Let that young lady know you're all right."

He nodded. He had a lot to tell Alice. Some of it tomorrow. Some would have to wait awhile longer—until after she'd done with wearing black. But the time would come. He was sure of that. He grinned slightly to himself, certain of what her answer would be.

We hope that you enjoyed reading this
Sagebrush Large Print Western.
If you would like to read more Sagebrush titles,
ask your librarian or contact the Publishers:

## United States and Canada

Thomas T. Beeler, *Publisher*
Post Office Box 659
Hampton Falls, New Hampshire 03844-0659
(800) 251-8726

## United Kingdom, Eire, and
## the Republic of South Africa

Isis Publishing Ltd
7 Centremead
Osney Mead
Oxford OX2 0ES  England
(01865) 250333

## Australia and New Zealand

Australian Large Print Audio & Video P/L
17 Mohr Street
Tullamarine, Victoria, 3043, Australia
1 800 335 364